The Veil of Silence

The Veil of Silence
Djura
Translated by Dorothy S. Blair

QUARTET BOOKS

First translated in English by Quartet Books Limited 1992
A member of the Namara Group
27/29 Goodge Street London W1P 1FD

First published in France by Editions Michel Lafon 1990

Copyright © by Djura 1990
Translation copyright © by Dorothy S. Blair 1992

British Library Cataloguing-in-Publication Data
Djura
 Veil of Silence
 I. Title II. Blair, Dorothy S.
 843.914 [F]

ISBN 0 7043 7033 6

Typeset by The Electronic Book Factory Ltd, Fife, Scotland
Printed and bound by
Bookcraft (Bath) Ltd

For Hervé and our son Riwan

Acknowledgements

To my friends on both sides of the Mediterranean,
to all those who have helped me with their
sympathy and friendship
I wish to express here my deepest gratitude.

I wish to thank from the bottom of my heart
Maître Isabelle Thery who has warmly
supported me in my final ordeals
and without whom this book
would not have seen the
light of day.

I pay a special tribute to
Huguette Maure who managed to polish my text,
with skill and sensitivity,
while always
respecting it.

The Text of Some of Djura's Songs

The author describes in her story how, at the performances given by DjurDjura, she explains in French the meaning of her songs, for the benefit of those in the audience who cannot understand the Berber language. The translator adds this *caveat* to the following verses: they are free and approximate English translations of the French version of some of the songs. They can only hope to convey something of Djura's subjects and preoccupations, such as she relates in her autobiography, without the possibility of rendering the rhythms and musicality of the Berber originals. 'Welcome Little Girl' is from DjurDjura's second album, entitled *Asirem,* meaning 'Hope', 'Norah' and 'I am Young' from the album *'A Yemma'.*

D.S.B.

Norah

This simple name is that of a sixteen-year-old girl killed by her family. It reminds us of the absurdity and intolerance of a tradition which chooses its victims amongst the weakest and most innocent.

> Norah, this letter I must write
> Although it cannot reach your eyes
> Where your buried body lies
> But thanks to you, we now unite
> To defend the future's youth
> We never cease to hear your cries,
> Repeated still from mouth to mouth,

East to West, North to South
Your memory shall endure
By this our song kept evergreen
Killed by your brothers, just sixteen,
Hard as it is to tell this truth . . .

To justify their crime
They invoked the usual claim:
'Ancestral law her death decreed
She went too far, she brought us shame.'

What we fear does come to pass
You die for a word, an idea, alas!
You were a flower in its prime
Norah, of beauty pure
Victim of a wicked deed
And in your heart: the beauty of the world . . .

For you and our sisters we shall sing
Mountains we shall move
Our words will be sharp and cutting,
They will uphold our dignity
Which many seek to disprove
Truth is a clear refreshing spring.

I am Young and I Want to Live

This song sums up the responsibility of every individual for the general evolution of people's mentalities.

I am not afraid, I want to sing
I am young and I want to live . . .
Listen, my friends, to this confession
I shall not beat about the bush

I shall tell you of a genuine nightmare
Which ever haunts me.
I still see their threatening knives
My feet were bound
And I could not restrain my tears.

I lay on the ground, and could not rise
They wanted my death.
I still don't know for what crime.
Only, our hopes were different.

I have tasted bitterness
Heard the vilest insults
But they are not alone in their guilt
My parents were in league with them.

You have pursued me even in my dreams
But you cannot break my will
I wait for the season of the figs, for better times.
Are you satisfied
Now that you have stolen my right to happiness?
I tell you today
That I reject all authority
And that the conjugation of the word Woman is
Liberty . . .

Welcome, Little Girl

Welcome, little girl!
You who bring us peace.
When you were born
Your parents rejected you.
I wish you long life,
You are the one who brings happiness.

Welcome to you, my daughter!
You used to go to fetch the water
You used to be the maid-of-all-work
Indispensible in the home.
My daughter, life has changed,
You are now the equal of your brothers.

Welcome, little girl!
Partridge perched so high
You whom I cherished, protected.
I reared you in the harsh November months
To see you grow
And exist.

Welcome to you, little girl!
You who bring us peace.
In former times, according to tradition
Your mother only wanted a boy
Fortunately all has changed,
Today is a new day.

Welcome little girl!
You, for whom I suffered so much
I bore you nine months in my womb
Just like your brother.
My daughter, for all the good that I did you
Perhaps in the evening of my life you will remember.

Welcome to you, little girl!
Today is a holiday
Good fortune is written on your brow
And your destiny is clear.
We shall fire rifle-shots for you
Just as we did for your brother
Henceforth, your birth shall be a day of rejoicing.

The following story is my story. However, it would never have occurred to me to write it, if events had not taken such a dramatic turn that it became urgent to exorcize the past.

Up till now, a veil of modesty discreetly masked the pain and suffering inflicted on me. In my songs I only disclosed my hope for better conditions for so many women in the world who still endure the crushing yoke of an outdated 'tradition'.

The drama which occurred, as well as what other women confided in me at the end of my performances, made me realize that my fate – exceptional as it may appear – was also, in part, that of thousands of girls, sisters or wives, who keep silent out of fear, who seek a decent life while they are forbidden even to exist.

In agreeing to tell my story, I wished to lift this veil of silence, so that a day might come when we could see the end of this masquerade which justifies itself on the grounds of ancestral customs but which has no longer any legitimacy – in the human sense of the word.

29 June 1987, one o'clock . . . The weather is scorching hot, the banks of the Seine are deserted. Generally the barge owners make the most of the fine weather to paint their boats, but today no-one dares touch the burning hulls. Our barge is motionless, everything here is peaceful.

Hervé isn't very hungry, neither am I. We make do with a mixed salad and half a pineapple, that we eat in the hold of our floating home, which we have just converted into a sort of kitchenette, thirties style. A magnificent mahogany counter, unearthed in a flea-market, a blue bench and two bistro-type tables are our main items of furniture.

I am wearing a floral Kabyle gown, which hangs loosely on my seven-months pregnancy. I can feel the baby moving, I make the most of this moment, I can scarcely believe it is happening. To bring into the world the child of the man you love! For many women that may seem the simplest thing in the world: for me, it is the culmination of a struggle, the realization of a dream that yesterday I still thought beyond my reach.

The doctor who did the echogram said, 'Your baby's a jumper!' His father and I laughed . . .

While we are finishing our lunch, we hear vague footsteps on the deck. We don't have time to react: the

The Veil of Silence

door is flung open, A man bursts in. I barely have time to recognize him than his revolver is already thrust into my belly. He pushes me violently against the counter, then hurls himself at Hervé and beats him about the head with the butt of the revolver. At this moment a girl rushes in, flings herself at me, grabs hold of me, kicking and punching me all over. She swears at me, pulls my hair, then goes for my belly which I try to protect as best I can.

'I'm pregnant!' I scream.

'So what?' she sneers, still raining blows on me.

I am rendered speechless with stupefaction, panic, fear of losing my baby. In spite of my unwieldy body, I try to reach the stairs that lead to the outside, but this she-devil furiously blocks my way.

Suddenly I hear a shot. The man must have fired at Hervé who he has chased on to the deck above. Terrified, I try once more to get off the boat and call for help. But the girl pushes me hard and I fall down the stairs.

I can't manage to get to my feet. The man rushes back down the stairs in front of me, calling his accomplice.

'Sabine, come on, hurry!'

They tear up the stairs, the man wearing a black leather bomber jacket, the girl also dressed all in black, including her tights. Later, I wonder about this colour, in midsummer. Is it to hide the blood that has splashed on to them? Bloodstains don't show up so much on a dark background . . .

I daren't stand up. I feel I shall go into labour immediately I try to get up. I drag myself to the telephone, holding my belly in both hands and dial 17, to call the police. Then I summon all my courage and manage to get to my feet and reach the deck. A frightful sight awaits me: Hervé is staggering along the embankment, covered with red gashes. He looks like an animal which has just been bled and which will die any minute. For my part I know that,

The Veil of Silence

even if I manage to save my baby, something in me has just died. My whole life collapsed, on the Seine, at one o'clock in the afternoon of 29 June 1987.

For the people who came to attack us were none other than my brother Djamel and my niece Sabine, and I knew that they acted on orders from the family.

When I woke up the next day in hospital, my face, arms and legs were a mass of bruises. My head weighed a ton, I hurt all over, I was afraid. The police had arrived very quickly, to find the barge one pool of blood. I had been taken to hospital and given sedatives.

Now I was fighting back. The uterine contractions could be seen on the monitor, strong and repeated. My child! My child in danger . . . I talked to him as if he had already been born: 'Hold on, be tough, my baby!' I stroked him gently, through my skin, thinking of the first echogram, in which I had seen his tiny hand, five fingers stretched out as if in greeting. Thinking of the time when I believed I was starting a new existence, protected from our tradition of summary justice . . .

Today my child was threatened, Hervé had lost so much blood that I feared the worst for him, and my passion for life gave way to a flood of tears.

The doctor prescribed anti-spasmodics and complete rest. I ought to stay in bed until I came to term. She insisted on keeping me in hospital, guessing I would not be safe anywhere else.

'But this isn't my home! I can't hide like this for ever!' I protested helplessly.

She smiled sadly. 'What do you think! Life isn't a bed of roses for an Algerian woman, and a singer into the bargain . . . The next time I see you on television, I'll think of you.'

The Veil of Silence

That comforted me. She was the first sympathetic person I'd met since the drama. But I still wept endlessly. Wept for the absurdity of it all.

The absurdity of women's situation, which for some is still mediaeval, even those living under western skies preparing for the second millenium. The absurdity of the traditions which inspire my music and songs, to be sure, but which I try to bring up to date, while customs persist in clinging to a criminal, outmoded sense of female 'honour', and for which I have paid the price, like so many girls of my race, at the risk of my life.

My life . . . My beloved country, the flowers of the Djurdjura Mountains, my family who I have cared for, cherished, and yet who hate me, who are unable to accept my love of art and my simple need of freedom. My life which, on this hospital bed where I fought to save a little creature, so that he should not become another victim – my life, which I had plenty of time to re-enact in my memory, my life overcast with violence and tears, but to which smiles and hope also never failed to bring sunshine.

'When the good Lord sneezes, he scatters narcissi', so goes a poem from our country. Every springtime, God floods my native village, Ifigha, with them – Ifigha which huddles high on a hilltop, at the foot of the Djurdjura Mountains.

Djurdjura, *montus ferratus*, the iron mountain, as the Romans called it, doubtless on account of the pride, courage, stubborn resistence, hidden in these rugged crags. This difficult countryside decks out its poverty with sumptuous scenery. Its hills, ravines and rivers, its fig plantations and its plains, in which the tree of peace predominates – the olive-tree with its glistening leaves – shelter a people who never submit, never bend the knee to anyone: the Kabyles. Berbers . . .

Beneath their exquisite manners and acute sense of hospitality they fiercely conceal their fundamental nature: unfailing dignity, unwavering respect for traditional values and a deep-seated attachment to the soil of their ancestors. Barbary – the land of the Berbers – claims its inhabitants to be a pure race. In fact, they are a mixture of Greeks, Sicilians, Andalusians, Africans, Provençals, Turks and other Mediterranean peoples who landed on the coast, century after century, and married or raped the local

The Veil of Silence

women, according to the conqueror at the time. Here are to be seen people who are tall with light blue eyes, others small with brown eyes, nomads and sedentary folk, archaism side by side with modernism, the East with the West. Successive waves of pagans, Christians, Jews, Muslims have made this region into a separate mosaic, curiously united against everything that comes from without. Berber and rebellious, such is the land I come from.

Berber and rebellious, like the little girl I was, the adolescent I became, the woman that I am.

Like Queen Kahina, whose fate awakens strange echoes in me. History tells us that her father, King Tabat, treated the little Dehya (that was Kahina's name at that time) with the greatest contempt, furious that his wife Birzil had not given him a son who would succeed him as chief of the Berber tribes.

To win her father's love, Dehya went every day to pray to the sacred ram to change her into a boy. In vain. Then she decided to be like a man by learning to use the weapons of the period. Her friend Zenon, a young Greek, taught her to shoot with bow and arrow. She soon showed such skill, such eagerness to do battle that, on the death of King Tabat, the people appointed her to succeed him.

The Kabyles in the past appreciated the pleasures of life. Prudery, severe laws concerning women did not emerge till the nineteenth century, as a reaction against the West and colonization. At the time of King Tabat, customs were much freer and girls ventured to behave quite shamelessly. Those who wore the most ankle-bracelets, which indicated the number of lovers they had attracted, were the most appreciated. Dehya wore many anklets and, without marrying Zenon, she bore him a child.

Besides the warriors of her tribes, the new queen had formed an army of horsewomen, ready to follow

The Veil of Silence

her without flinching into the battles which she waged against the Arab invader. Her instinct and a certain gift for prophecy helped her to triumph over her enemies who gave her the nickname of *Kahina*: the prophetess or, more disparagingly, the sorceress.

At first the Berber people adored her. Then, doubtless nostalgic for masculine authority, they forced her to take a husband in order to have a king, a genuine one, a man. Kahina had her revenge for this affront by marrying the oldest, the ugliest, the most tyrannical of her suitors. You wanted a chief, well now you've got one!

Immediately her husband inaugurated a reign of terror, of injustice, inflicting misery, exacting submission. Before very long the people were demanding the return of the queen. Disgusted by her husband's machinations, Kahina chastised him in the public square. Unfortunately he had given her a son who took after his father in every respect, double-dealing, cruel, dangerous.

Nevertheless she resumed command of the army, speeding from victory to victory . . . Unfortunately again, she became infatuated with a young prisoner, whom she adopted in order to protect him. Following the current ritual, she stood at the top of the royal staircase, unfastened her tunic and publicly offered her breast to the young man, thus raising him to the rank of her own descendants. Only this young man was no other than the nephew of the great Uqba, the leader of the Arab armies. Although he was grateful to Kahina for having saved him, he was nonetheless determined to massacre the Berbers and their beloved sorceress.

In fact it was the legitimate son of the queen herself who facilitated his task, by betraying his mother's military secrets to her enemies.

Kahina lost ground, but with every retreat she burned the land behind her, rather than let it fall intact into the hands of the invader. Gradually her warriors abandoned her, uttering the expected cries of '*Allahu Akbar*', 'Allah is great'. Only the army of women continued to support her to the end, before she allowed herself to be killed, leaving the field free to the enemy.

That is how the Barbary of the Romans, the kingdom ruled over successively by Massinissa, Jugurtha, then by Kahina, became the *Ifriqiya* of the Arabs, the name deriving from the root 'frq' which means, according to Calif Omar, division, separation, splitting.

The Arabs had, it seems, well understood the ambiguous nature of this people: brave and united at its great moments, but torn by tribal struggles, internal quarrels, family rivalry. That has not changed, in spite of Kahina, who was never subjugated, Kahina whom I admire for her single-mindedness and who has been my role model each time I have had, like her, a struggle to follow my path, in the teeth of the treachery of my own family, whose happiness I had thought to have assured. Kahina was, like me, the cause of deep disappointment at her birth, because she was a girl . . .

I was a girl, sure enough, and my village would have no celebrations to mark my coming into the world. My fortress-village, built like so many similar ones in Kabylia, to turn its back on the outside world. My village with its tiled roofs, its stones assembled with clay, its rough, bumpy roads.

I can still see it, such as it appeared to me in my childhood, at the beginning of the fifties . . . Situated more than 120 miles north-east of Algiers, past the famous Yakouren forest, at over 3000 feet altitude, Ifigha remains a secret. The main roads avoid it, strangers scarcely ever

The Veil of Silence

come there. A wide track, lined with eucalyptus trees, I remember, led to the central square.

On the left stood the headquarters of the French army, now the post office. On the right, the café. I still have imprinted on my memory the picture of men sitting at tables in front of a glass of tea, sometimes for a whole day on end. With their burnous pulled up over their shoulders, they would twirl their moustaches with one hand, clutching their tins of *chema* – chewing tobacco – in the other, while discussing the thousands of rumours that circulated in the mountains. Some of them played *rounda*, a Spanish card game, very popular in Algeria, others played dominoes . . . In front of the café, the old men in their turbans sat on the ground in the shade of a tree, or leaned against a wall, resting on a shepherd's stick as gnarled as themselves in their old age, and voiced their disarming fatalism in brief commonplaces: '*El-qarn arváatac*, the end of this century will be terrible, it's written in the books.' Or else: '*O! Djil n'toura!* Oh! the young people nowadays . . .' Or simply, '*Mektoub*, It's written'.

Not far from the café, a weatherbeaten general merchant sat in state on a low stool in front of his shop. Buckets, basins, shoes, brightly-coloured shiny plastic jugs overflowed onto the pavement. On the outside walls and in the shop-window were hung brooms, shovels, rugs, couscous steamers, enamel plates and dishes imported from China or other Eastern countries, as well as local pottery. Everything could be found here, from bottled gas to semolina, including spices, vegetables, fruit, matches and sweets. This merchant's family owned the mills and olive presses where olive-oil was extracted. He was one of the village notables.

This corner of the village was generally frequented by men. Women hurried past without turning their heads in the direction of the café. On Wednesdays they avoided the place, as it was market day, forbidden to women folk. Then the square was invaded by a horde of peasants of majestic bearing, come to make their purchases, exchange their produce and chat. The richest ones bought meat, which they deliberately let hang out of their baskets, out of a sort of innocent pride. A way of showing that they had just received a postal order from France and that, on the other side of the Mediterranean, a son or a brother was thinking of them. Many Kabyles had already left the village. Ifigha had even been called 'Little Paris', as a sort of tribute to all those who had emigrated to earn their living over there. When a letter arrived from these beloved exiles, there was a rush to find someone who could decipher it, translate the words, always the same, 'I hope that my letter finds you in good health . . . I have sent you a postal order . . . I am well, don't worry about me . . .'

The men would fold up the letter and go off to tell their wives, their sisters or their nieces, when the latter returned from fetching water. There is very little vegetation here, except for olives and figs. In order to eat vegetables and fruit, the vegetable garden has to be watered daily, and to that end water has to be fetched from the well in the middle of the village. That is a task exclusively reserved for females, and I can still see these proud girls, with tense necks, balancing full jars on their heads, without even using their hands.

These mountain women were fine plants, at least in their youth, before they were worn out with toil. Their long Kabyle gowns – *tiksiwin* – added as much colour to the landscape as the narcissi and the eucalyptus trees. These cotton or satin *tiksiwin* were embroidered with precious braids on the shoulders, wrists and sleeves. To protect them the countrywomen wrapped a *fouta* – a sort of red and gold striped cloth – round their waists to serve as an apron while they did the housework or worked in the

The Veil of Silence

fields. On their hair they wore the *amendil*, the traditional headscarf, into which they stuck narcissi, as much for the scent as for the white contrast which showed up their dark, deep-set, oriental eyes to advantage.

They gathered merrily at the well in the square, or at their own market, the women's market, swapping jewellery, splashing each other like kids, arguing or gossiping, while the village children scrapped around them. They talked in loud voices, accustomed as they were to calling to each other from one hill to another, just as I called when I was small to my friend Faroudja, making without realizing it, my first attempts to vocalize: 'Aaaaa-Faaarrouououououdjaaa . . .'

'Man and woman are like the sun and the moon. They see each other but they never meet', so goes the proverb. The men did not come to the women's market any more than girls entered the café or the mosque situated just opposite the well. Which didn't prevent the boys, on the threshold of the holy place, from delighting in the sight of the village girls at work, sometimes taking a fancy to one of them, with a view to a future marriage. All that seemed natural and at first I only saw the smiling – or folksy – side of things. The segregation of the sexes, the rigour of the customs, misplaced modesty, supremacy of the male, weighed heavily on these women's eyes which are called mysterious, no doubt because they express what the mouth cannot say: the burden of inequality endured since birth.

My birth . . . One third of April, at dawn. Someone said, 'It's good to be born in the morning, she will be brave and strong.'

My mother was devastated: she'd hoped for a boy. All

pregnant women hoped for boys. And the fathers, and the aunts, and the whole village! People waited for the yuyus, the cries of joy which greeted the arrival into this world of the male child. When yuyus were in order, the happy event was celebrated the same evening with drums and *reïtas* – instruments carried on the hip and which sound like mortars – and the celebratory couscous would be distributed all round. The absence of yuyus, on the contrary, meant that a girl had been born. The midwife herself felt exasperated by this feminine gender, this 'turnip' as they say in Tlemcen, this 'wood-louse' as they say in Saîda, this 'pumpkin' according to the inhabitants of Constantine. The father would slip away to the café to find consolation in the words of sympathy on all sides, 'Don't give up hope! Anyone who can have a daughter, can certainly have a son one day . . .' The young mother stayed at home, abandoned like a heap of dead ashes, terrified at the idea of not having a male heir, for then she ran the risk of being repudiated.

My mother had nothing of this sort to fear as she had already had a son, my elder brother Mohand – diminutive of Mohammed. When the first child is a boy, the wife feels her cup of joy running over. The baby will be made much of, coddled, breast-fed sometimes till he is five years old or more! The day of my arrival on earth, my mother was still suckling my brother, aged three and a half. Was this an excuse not to breast-feed me? I was the only one of her children to whom she refused her milk. From the morning of my birth, she rejected me. I should have remembered this, later, when I made so many sacrifices, in the vain and childish hope of winning her love . . .

And yet I was suckled! And yet the village did celebrate

The Veil of Silence

for me, little Djura, a negligable quantity up till the moment when the 'miracle' occurred.

My parents were living at this time with *Setsi* Fatima, that's to say 'grannie' Fatima, the wife of my paternal grandfather. In her youth Setsi Fatima had been a great beauty. Carrying herself like a queen, as graceful as a gazelle, with long plaits that hung down below her waist. The jewels, she wore in her ears, round her neck, on her arms, were no brighter than her turquoise eyes. Her white skin set off her perfect tattoos. She breathed good health, nobility, intelligence, and her serene face concealed an indomitable will.

But she had had much to put up with, as she was sterile: the worst of faults in our society. She had married several times, was appreciated by her husbands for her countless virtues, yet was each time repudiated for want of offspring. My grandfather was the only one not to leave her. He had been recruited into the French army, like so many others, to fight against the Germans, and on his return his wife was dead, leaving two young children: my father Saîd and my uncle Hamou. So my grandfather had looked for a nurse for his children, rather than a future mother. Therefore he agreed to marry Setsi Fatima, who brought up Saîd and Hamou.

Everyone loved Fatima, and it soon became apparent that, she compensated for being unable to bear children, by curing the others in the village of their daily ills. A heaven-sent gift? The fact is that, with her hands, a piece of string, some salt and faith, she did perform cures. People came from all directions to appeal to her generosity, her skill, her maternal instincts. She cut the cord of new-born babes, then she looked after them, invented games for them. The little tots called her *Djida*, another way of saying 'grandma'.

When she heard I was born – amid general gloom, as was

right and proper – she, for her part, experienced the greatest joy of her life. Was this the miracle of repressed maternal love? Her milk began to flow abundantly and after I had drunk my fill of the substance my mother refused me, she gently sprinkled it on my face, as newly-delivered mothers do to cleanse their babies.

When people heard the news, they came from all around, on foot or on donkeys, bearing gifts and good wishes, to give thanks for this gift from God. They watched with amazement to see Fatima open her *gandoura* and her milk spill out. For them, this woman had become a saint. They prostrated themselves at her feet, begging her to heal this sickness or that, and most especially to cure the sterility of this woman or that. Then they crowded round my cradle to see the object of this miracle.

From that moment everyone knew me as Setsi Fatima's daughter. She bestowed on me *ánaya*, her protection. For five radiant years we were inseparable.

Our whole family lived in one large house at the highest point in Ifigha. It consisted of a collection of ramshackle buildings round a central courtyard, a sort of patio, under which our ancestors rested. It is said here that, in order to rest in peace, the dead must be buried on the very spot where they were born . . .

The shacks that surrounded the courtyard were so many separate rooms. My parents occupied one of these. I slept with Setsi Fatima in the biggest one, which also served as a common utility room. Common is the right word: on one side was the byre where a cow and her calf slept, on the other side was the rest of the accommodation, separated by a low wall and three steps. Above the cowshed was a mezzanine, containing chests for storing clothes and other provisions. Below this, the space for the humans varied its function according to the time of day: kitchen, sewing-room, living-room, bedroom. In the evening, heavy woollen rugs were piled up, rugs woven by the women of the family in brightly coloured stripes or geometric patterns; these served as beds, and in the morning the rugs were hung over a wire in a corner, so that the place could be swept, and room made for our various activities.

Setsi Fatima was a force of nature. She left at dawn to fill the water jars, fetch wood and, in summer, pick fresh figs before the sun rose. I slept on much longer, until I was woken by the light of day, often opening my eyes to see a little bird twittering in front of the open door. After which I never left Setsi Fatima's side.

She had accustomed me from infancy, in fact, to being carried everywhere on her back, contrary to custom. On the whole, children here are not shown in public until they are six or seven months old, for fear of envious folk casting an evil eye on them. But I had been exhibited to the crowds from my first day, so one might as well continue! Soon however, seeing that I came home from our outings with violent headaches, Setsi Fatima decided to hang a few amulets round my neck to protect me.

Thus I became a real little princess, pampered, cosseted, showered with gifts. Setsi Fatima had white satin dresses made for me, embroidered with orange-blossom designs or tiny butterflies, set off with many-coloured trimmings. Before she dressed me in a new frock, she made me trample on it, as was the custom, while pronouncing the ritual Kabyle formula: 'Wear it out, before it wears you out!' I still do this with the Kabyle gowns I wear for all ocasions – public or private – and that I now make myself.

In the evening, by the fireside, (the winter nights are cold), Setsi Fatima told me local legends, sometimes subtly

The Veil of Silence

designed to teach me to be obedient, like saying. 'If you're not good, a sorceress will come and put you in a sack and throw you in the sea.' I believed this all the more as there was a genuine sorceress in the village. At least, that's what they called her: *Tseryel*, the sorceress . . . This woman had lost her wits on seeing her son die under her eyes. Since then she rambled incoherently. She often stopped in front of the mosque, took off her clothes and began to howl. Nobody intervened, this was in the order of things. There were no asylums; the mentally deficient, idiots, those suffering from every type of mental disorder, were not excluded from our society. People even held these roaming madmen dear, as God was said to cherish them.

All the same I was terrified of Tseryel. As soon as I could totter around by myself, I would make wide circuits to avoid her. Yet she and Setsi Fatima got on well. One day, when my grandmother was carrying me around on her shoulders, Tseryel offered me some grapes which I daren't taste for fear they were poisoned. Another time she approached me kindly, covered with dangling trinkets, safety-pins fastened to her dress, tin-cans by way of jewellery, and asked for an egg to foretell my future . . . She must have been wrong: it seems my future was to be – uneventful and radiant.

At all events my first discoveries of the wonderful world of entertainment were radiant – thanks to Setsi Fatima. She could be said to have put me on the stage at the age of four. Oh! not the stage of a proper theatre! The natural stage of Kabyle festivities. At that time there was no radio, not to mention television. People set the gala mood themselves, singing and dancing and beating empty oil-drums. Fatima bequeathed to me a sense of

The Veil of Silence

celebration. Everything was an excuse for rejoicing and everyone made the most of it, doing an act, singing or dancing. We children already imitated the actions of the women who dressed like empresses, however poor they might be in their daily lives.

The ceremony which made the greatest impression on me was the wedding of one of my aunts. A ceremonial wedding, beautiful as a promise, treacherous as the young bride's future . . .

The day before her wedding, the future bride was taken in hand by women of the village, professional beauticians, specializing in making skin soft as silk, painting hands and feet like miniatures. The day of the wedding ceremony, her face was transformed: kohl applied round her eyes, bright pink rouge on her cheeks, her eyebrows skilfully re-drawn, her gums and lips rubbed with *ayoussim*, walnut bark, to give them a sensual, attractive red-brown colour.

Then she was dressed in the traditional white gown, even more richly embroidered than usual, over which she wore a second sleeveless *gandoura*, with sumptuous trimming down the front. Enamelled and silver jewels adorned her arms, ears and ankles. Finally, the ceremonial necklace was placed round her neck. This consisted of three or four strings of yellow, green, gold and silver glass beads. Cloves carefully threaded between the beads gave off a heady scent: the aphrodisiac 'bouquet' of every young bride. On her head, large brooches secured the black fringed *amendil* over which another veil was placed to hide her face, which was only uncovered when she arrived at her husband's home.

A husband whom she had not chosen; her parents decided her fate, just as mine tried later to decide what I should do with my life.

A whole procession accompanied the bride to her new

home. The men wearing their best white burnouses, the women in their best finery . . . The musicians followed with their nasal-sounding *reītas*, their *tbels, bendirs* and *derboukas*, a variety of drums each with its different sound. Shots fired from the *baroud* – the Berber rifle – rang out on all sides. Hard-boiled eggs were thrown up into the air, just as in Europe rice, confetti or sugared almonds are thrown at the bridal pair. People caught the eggs in the air and ate them as they walked. At the end of the procession came mules laden with mattresses, household linen, hand-made rugs and carpets: the girl's trousseau.

Before she entered her husband's house, that is, her in-laws' home, the bride had to step over a stick, placed on the threshold. Then her father-in-law threw the stick on to the roof. If the stick stayed there, this was a good omen for them all: the future wife would be perfectly docile and submissive. If it fell down, they began to look at her askance: you'd have to look out for this girl.

Then the revelry began. Food and drink was distributed. The *medah*, a popular poet, complimented the husband, the wife, the groom's mother, father, in-laws and friends in a pompous, theatrical speech, punctuated by the women's approving cries. There was endless dancing and singing. It is from that time that I have retained my nostalgia for those high-pitched female voices, those shrill incantations, obsessive rhythms and symbolic gestures that I have tried to re-introduce to the stage in my performances, if for no other reason than to enlighten those who think North African choreography only consists of the belly dance for tourists.

The festivities lasted for seven days and seven nights. Everyone kept their eyes glued to the young bride. A

The Veil of Silence

veritable ceremonial accompanied her first expedition to fetch water: the other wives helped her, gave her advice. The bride changed her outfit every day, making herself more and more beautiful to please her husband. Then her real life as a woman began: she saw less and less of her parents, she had to prove herself up to everything demanded of her, ask 'her-majesty-the-mother-in-law' permission for her slightest action. Sometimes she still smiled, happy among understanding people; at other times, her expression clouded over and she secretly cursed her parents who had delivered her into a hostile world without asking her opinion.

At that time, I was four or five, and my only memory of this official subservience was the entertainment provided for my earliest years.

I was not aware either of the difficulties that my parents encountered. Both came from respectable families, so-called 'landed proprietors'. The expression was rather grand for the ownership of a few small olive groves or fig plantations, but these sufficed to indicate that we belonged to the rural gentry.

My father had even had the luck to be educated in French, which was a privilege at that time, only ten per cent of Algerian children of his generation having had any schooling. Despite that, he couldn't manage to find extra work to help maintain his family.

The fields were not enough, in fact, to provide for our subsistence. My mother had just had another daughter, my sister Fatima, whom she was prepared to breast-feed, as my brother was now . . . five and a half. Mohand was already a little terror, spoilt, unruly, accustomed to getting his own way in everything. Three

The Veil of Silence

children already . . . My father tried in vain to find a job and gradually the idea of leaving for France came to fruition.

At the beginning of the fifties, France strongly encouraged immigration which supplied cheap labour. There was a massive exodus of Kabyles, who were particularly poor. Anyone who had a cousin or brother already living in France left to join them, leaving wife and children behind until they had enough money to send for them. The women, left all alone in Kabylia, complained, calling France 'the man-eater'. They waited for the money-orders, the letters, the 'don't-worry-about-me, everything's-fine-here' . . . For his part, the expatriate, ex-landed proprietor, accepted every humiliation, like a nobleman down on his luck: illegal employment, precarious housing, insecurity, isolation for him as well.

My father had cousins settled in Paris who worked in restaurants, cafés, cheap hotels. They encouraged him to come to France and one day he left to cross the sea . . . From the very next day after his departure, we began to wait for his return. At every meal his spoon was there ready in the big dish of couscous. But he did not come and we ate gloomily in silence.

To tell the truth, I was much less upset than the others. I had Setsi Fatima, my outings with her, her songs and laughter, the first fig she offered me in the morning, saying, 'Here, eat and grow big, O my bright shining rose!'

I was fair-complexioned with dark curly hair, and black mischievous eyes, so I am told. Setsi Fatima had nicknamed me *Jouhjouh Henina*, plaything of love . . . I think I learned everything from her: her courage, her strength, but also – unfortunately perhaps – a certain fatalism and a tendency to sacrifice oneself, which was nearly my undoing . . .

The Veil of Silence

Three years elapsed, during which my father came back to see us once. He regularly sent us money, he wrote, he was sorry – like the other expatriates – not to see his children grow up. It was a vicious circle: the men returned to Algeria for short holidays, begat more babies, left for France again to work to bring up an increasingly large family, which however they scarcely knew. My father could no longer accept this separation. What is more, in November 1954, the first shots in the Algerian War had been fired in the Aures mountains. Large numbers of Maquisards were taking refuge in the Djurjura mountains, following in the footsteps of Kahina the Rebel Queen. We were no longer safe. This caused my father to decide all the faster to bring us to Paris, notwithstanding the discomfort of his lodgings.

December 1954 . . . I can remember my despair at the idea of leaving Setsi Fatima. I was old enough to realize what I was leaving behind. I was losing everything which made for my security. I knew that my mother preferred my brother, and also little Fatima. As for my father, I had seen so little of him that I scarcely knew him. I left sorrowfully, not sharing Mother's joy.

Like all the women who went off to join their husbands in France, she was really delighted, expecting to arrive in a land of milk and honey. This myth, moreover, was carefully preserved by the immigrants themselves who came back on holiday with suitcases filled with shoddy gifts, but which made a good impression. The girls in Ifigha even went so far as to exchange their sumptuous satins for vulgar Parisian rayons, and their traditional jewellery for paste, with no value and no beauty, but which sparkled and came from a land of riches.

I couldn't care less about this land of luxury. I was going off into the unknown, I was afraid and I was suffering. Suffering at the loss of my benefactress, my good fairy,

The Veil of Silence

my real mother as far as the heart was concerned. I can still see myself snatched from her arms while, with eyes filled with tears, she pronounced these words heavy with foreboding for the future:

'Goodbye, my daughter, go towards your destiny . . .'

It was the first time I had seen the sea. My first experience of the sea, which was particularly rough. We travelled steerage, packed together like cattle. Everyone slept on the floor. People were seasick, including myself. We spent the whole crossing in this atmosphere of heaving bodies, floundering in vomit. The air was full of a nauseating, unbearable stench. The arrival at Marseilles, in the grey light, was a release.

My father had bought my mother a black and white check costume. He was anxious for her to disembark dressed like a Frenchwoman. This was something new for her, as she'd never worn anything except Kabyle gowns. She must have felt restricted in that tight skirt and jacket nipped in at the waist, fifties style. I watched her as we went through all the landing formalities before catching the train for Paris. I thought her beautiful, I loved her, I wanted her to love me, I think . . .

In Paris, we took the Metro from the Gare de Lyon to Belleville, to a little furnished hotel room in the Faubourg-du-Temple, where my father was living. We stayed there more than two years. This room was very cramped and the only light came from a window so tiny I thought it was a skylight. Through this skylight, where no

The Veil of Silence

bird came to greet me when I woke, I could see huge walls rising up everywhere. The outside world disconcerted me. Where were the big fields that I crossed to go and help Setsi Fatima do the washing in the river? The landscape here seemed artificial, like badly erected scenery. The street concealed a thousand perils. I had never seen so many cars and people out-of-doors, in such a hurry . . .

During our stay in the Faubourg-du-Temple, my mother hardly ever went out. Not speaking a word of French, she didn't even go shopping. A neighbour did it for her, accompanied by her dog Kelly, an impressive black greyhound who bit anyone in uniform – postmen, policemen and bus-drivers – plus a few others, including my brother and sister. Fortunately I was spared.

Before long mother gave birth to another boy, of whom she was obviously very proud. The family was growing and the room seemed to shrink proportionately. I found mother sad, disappointed, resigned. My father treated her badly. I remember seeing him hit her for the first time one evening because the dinner wasn't ready. That shook me. Yet, in Kabylia, men often raised their hands to their wives at the slightest thing that displeased them. But perhaps it was less noticeable for the children, in our large low houses with their scattered buildings.

Here, on the other hand, nothing could escape us, with six people in one room. My mother's life was concentrated into these few square yards: the baby, the nappies, the washing, cooking, cleaning, putting down makeshift beds on the floor in the evening, like back home in Algeria, but with much less room and nothing beautiful outside. Never, in Ifigha, could I have imagined living in such conditions.

Fortunately my father had entered Mohand and me in school, which gave us an opportunity of getting out of our dump. I began to learn French and also to judge the

The Veil of Silence

difference between me and Parisian children. I felt isolated. In the evening I tried to draw nearer to mother, who had other things to do than to listen to me. Father, with the help of a welfare organization, had applied for rehousing. After two years it was suggested that we go to live in the thirteenth *arrondissement* . . .

57 boulevard Masséna: damp, prefabricated huts, not very salubrious. Social Services had explained that this was an emergency housing estate, temporary housing while waiting for something better. This 'temporary' lasted eight years for us, but we couldn't complain. Other immigrants lived in much more wretched shantytowns. We had running water, electricity, two fair-sized rooms: luxury!

The huts were arranged in three parallel blocks, the whole lot surrounded by wire netting, like at the zoo. Our immediate neighbours on the right were charming black Muslims who never gave any trouble; on the left was the person in charge of the estate – a Frenchwoman – with her husband and two children. Other members of the French sub-proletariate had also taken refuge here: the Nonos family, who had built a sort of extension-shack out of empty drums and pieces of wood to help house their innumerable offspring; Mimi and Lulu, the two dwarfs who spent their time drinking red wine out of cracked bottles. Their house was always full of drunkards like themselves and at night quarrels broke out. Then we shut doors and windows as bottles flew around outside, as well as crockery and anything they could lay their hands on. They fought like Kilkenny cats, but the next morning they were friends once more and resumed their drinking . . . Lulu had a daughter Micky, a platinum blonde with bright red lips who thought herself a Marilyn Monroe in

The Veil of Silence

her tight skirt and practised, I think, the oldest profession in the world.

The Russians were much more discreet. They lived at the end of the third block, a little further away. A father and his two children, mad about classical music and relatively cultivated. However had they landed up here? I've no idea.

However, the estate was inhabited mostly by North Africans. Halima, from Oran, with the undersized, imperturbable husband, was the only woman who laid down the law in her own home . . . My friend Fanny lived in the first row: her mother looked like a film star, always elegantly dressed, with short hair stylishly cut, and refined manners. Everyone thought she was a Parisian from a smart district, especially as she spoke impeccable French, without a trace of accent. It's true she'd been living in France for more than thirty years. For me, Fanny and the women of her family represented the elite of our microcosm. This was not the opinion of the other Muslims in the place, who thought these ladies too sophisticated: Western coquetry and elegance for them being synonymous with loose living.

Customs had scarcely evolved, in fact, and women still remained under the more or less strict masculine yoke. Not far from Fanny, a Tunisian literally prevented his wife from showing her face out of doors. Sometimes the poor woman could be seen at her window, dreaming like a prisoner . . . Abdallah, the father of Khalima – another of my friends – had brought back from Algeria, after his wife's death, a girl of eighteen, whom he'd married. He was getting on for sixty. His son Bachir, by his first wife, was the same age as his stepmother, and people gossiped about this discreet girl who had strayed into a bed of another generation. What is more, Abdallah seemed completely round the bend: every morning, by way of greeting, he bit his daughter Khalima

The Veil of Silence

on the thigh, just like that, quite openly but kindly. Don't ask me why . . . Aïssa, an alcoholic, unemployed Kabyle, regularly beat his better half, who rushed out of the house screaming. Then he chased after her with an axe shouting, '*Din ou qavach*! In the name of the axe!' Eventually he cracked her skull . . . Amokrane treated his family no less gently. His weapon was his belt, and every evening screams of pain could be heard coming from his hut.

True, all the North African children seemed used to putting up with their father's violent authority. We were no exception to the rule, only I could not get used to it. We were one of the most respectable families in the estate: I couldn't understand this outrageous brutality. Our parents did their best to bring us up decently and were very concerned that both boys and girls should have a primary education. But at the slightest bad mark, we got a good hiding. I was terrified of my father's reactions. When my weekly report was only average, I panicked so much that I peed in my pants.

Yet I think he was fond of me. Occasionally he brought my sister and me splendid gifts, such as the magnificent plaid costume that he gave me one year for the Feast of the Sheep, while Fatima was presented with a lovely salmon-pink dress. That being said, moments of affection were rare: no doubt there were too many of us. I can only recall two marks of attention: the shower-bath my father gave me, one morning, in a large basin of water, placed on the squatting lavatory, amid shrieks of laughter; and the sweets he brought me one evening to make me forget the violent toothache which kept me in bed. It was almost worth having toothache every day . . .

My mother, like all Algerian women of her generation, put up with her husband, as she had been ordered to do. She hadn't chosen her spouse either. She had even run away from the marital home several times when she was young,

The Veil of Silence

soon to be brought back to the fold. After Mohand was born, she stayed put. Pregnancies had followed fast on each other. By 1956, she was at her fifth. In all she has had nine children, five boys and four girls.

All of us from North Africa had very large families, with eight, ten, or even fifteen children. When outside people asked how many we were, we evaded the truth. As soon as we mentioned the number, it was not unusual for them to reply maliciously, 'Your mothers breed like rabbits! They keep on having brats they're incapable of feeding.'

But what could the poor 'rabbits' do? The pill didn't exist. Even if it had, the husbands would have had none of it. Their children were their capital. They thought they'd work for them later, since they themselves were still supporting their parents. Offspring, in our tradition, are 'what God has given us': a divine fatality, at the same time as an investment for one's old age. How could the French understand that?

In any case, for the French, there was nothing to understand. We were poor, we were wretched, a people apart, who they shouldn't mix with. 'Frightful, dirty, wicked', like people in a film by Ettore Scola, despised by the outside world, dangerous savages. In the 'Parisian' block of flats that overlooked our estate, the tenants were constantly at their windows, looking down on this spectacle of outlandish riffraff, as if it were an entertainment. They called it the free cinema, looking forward to the next showings, laughing to see us Arabs, Wogs, roughing each other up. I called us 'The Wog Family', parodying a radio serial popular at the time.[1] Thus we learned the meaning

---

[1] The radio serial in question was 'La famille Duraton'. The author makes a running word play on the name of the French family, as the vulgar, racist term for Arab immigrants in French (equivalent to 'Wog') is *raton*, literally 'little rat'. (Trans.)

The Veil of Silence

of social classes, which we found reassuring to some extent: we couldn't fall any lower.

This humiliating difference was the source of real solidarity among us. We shared our solitude, no matter how different we might be from each other. We exchanged visits, joined in the celebration of feast days, each one bringing cakes or other food. Life taught us to makeshift, not to be stupid, never bow our heads or lower our arms: we were proud! It may be asked, what did we have to be proud of, but we kept our dignity, in spite of our folksy ways. The Algerian War tightened our links, bringing to the expatriates a feeling of naïve hope, as if their situation would be miraculously transformed the day they won their independence.

In my mind, as a child, this war didn't have any very clear meaning, except an instinctive revolt against injustice, against our misery and exclusion. As for independence, already as a little girl going on seven, I was struggling for mine, without knowing it. I had formed a very united, very tough gang of little friends, of which I was the leader. Among ourselves, we spoke a curious mixture of Arabic, Kabyle and French, the same as the adults. I organized the games, which were never violent. I imagined I was Kahina, whose story Setsi Fatima had told me. The street was our domain. As long as I was small, my parents let me play around outside; this left more room in the house. Which doesn't mean that no-one kept an eye on me: my eldest brother had the job of keeping me to the straight and narrow. Moreover, even the youngest males were entrusted with authority over us girls. Mothers could be seen giving their youngest son a stick to beat his big sister with, others would hold the girl down while the devoted brother dutifully inflicted the chastisement. In spite of the fact that these women had themselves had to suffer from this state of affairs, they perpetuated the custom, inciting

The Veil of Silence

their sons to terrorize females, to develop their violence, their 'virility', to make 'men' of them. 'For you to become *izem*, my son: a lion.'

Mohand took full advantage of his birthright. He hit me in front of the members of my gang, which was particularly humiliating, as you can imagine. Sometimes he ordered me home roughly, chasing after me with kicks. One evening I had to escape through a window and hide outside the house waiting for my father to come back: Mohand in a rage had tried to break a bottle over my head. But neither my father nor my mother blamed him: I was the one who was punished. We were brought up to respect the older one who was always in the right, no matter what happened. My brother, without doing a thing, filled me with terror. One glance from his black eyes, and I'd clam up or take to my heels. I got my own back by exercising power elsewhere, with my pals.

Apart from Mohand, I wasn't frightened of any boys at that time. Neither the kids in my gang, nor the Parisian youngsters who re-enacted the Algerian war at the school gates. They pointed at us, shouting, 'Here comes French Algeria!' And we retorted, 'We're Algerian Algeria', and thumbed our noses at them.

Then we laid into them, settling our childish scores, with what looked like political awareness, but was really just letting off steam, and our way of rebelling against poverty.

Meanwhile, we spoke less and less Arabic or Kabyle, we went to watch cloak-and-dagger films at the only one of our neighbour's who had a television, and when we young 'Wogs' fought among ourselves, armed with sticks for swords, we were Fanfan-the-Tulip, the Knights of the Round Table or the Three Musketeers. Goodbye Kahina, no more sorceresses from the mountains of Kabylia, or legends of the Djurdjura mountains: we had changed

The Veil of Silence

heroes, and whilst our uncles back home were driving out the French, in order to become completely Algerian, we children, born in Algeria but living in France, were becoming more and more French.

In Paris, too, our parents were involved in the war. My father was a staunch militant member of the FLN – the Algerian Front for National Liberation – like many other men living in the estate. For us that meant, from 1954, regular house-searches, round-ups, Arab-bashing, permanent insecurity.

Up till now my father had been used to meeting his cousins in various Algerian cafés. But these places were well-known as haunts of the Resistance, so he preferred to keep away from them to avoid being picked up, and he took a job with Renault. He became more and more actively involved with the FLN, as did my maternal uncles who had come to live with us. Every evening we waited impatiently, afraid they would not return home. Members of the FLN were kept under close surveillance, arrested, imprisoned. Some simply disappeared. Their bodies were said to have been thrown into the Seine.

My father was arrested in 1959; they came for him with the handcuffs while he was working on the Renault assembly line. He had been denounced. He spent several months in the Fresnes prison, without trial, then was transferred to the Larzac camp, where we travelled on the Micheline rail-car to see him. Every time we visited him we were searched, things that we took him were minutely examined, all gifts of food being forbidden. I was in despair at seeing Papa in this pitiful place. Then I was in depair at not seeing him at all, as visits were suppressed.

The Veil of Silence

A few months later, we learned he'd been sent back to his own home in Algeria, under house arrest like other political prisoners. He was to stay there for three years.

My mother received a small allowance for us children from the FLN; my uncles provided for the rest of our expenses, according to an understood law of mutual assistance, which everyone respected in our vast tribes. My father's absence was to make a considerable change in his wife's existence. She finally acquired a certain independence. She gradually learned French and went to do her shopping with the other women from the estate. She used me as interpreter for administrative formalities, as the legal expressions were still too much for her. These applications to Social Security, for Family Allowances, and other public services became more and more difficult. There was always a form that had been wrongly filled up or that was missing. I was naturally responsible for doing all the writing – and even for signing – as my mother couldn't write. We had to go back time and time again, instead of getting all the documents for our case completed once and for all, and we wasted entire days in queues, waiting for our names to be called. When our turn arrived, the clerks behind the counter received us coldly, niggling over minute details, and all that time, I was thinking of the classes I was missing.

My father wrote to us regularly, enjoining his wife to behave properly. Was he jealous? However, no-one could have imagined my mother with another man! On the other hand, cousins and friends claimed that he did not deprive himself of affairs, back home. All this was half-suggested, leaving me perplexed, in view of my youth.

On the contrary, there was nothing equivocal about my

The Veil of Silence

father's return to Paris, immediately after the Algerian cease-fire. Was it the result of his imprisonment, then his exile, or this long separation, or perhaps my mother's relative emancipation? He became aggressive, much more violent than in the past, suspicious of his wife. Finally he took to drink and our martyrdom began.

When he was drunk he flew into terrible rages and laid into my mother blindly. He was unrecognizable. Although he had always been harsh, before he became an alcoholic, he was a respectable, good man. But from now on, he took every opportunity of attacking mother, whom I defended, although I was only twelve and she showed me little affection. Then I also got beaten unmercifully. My brother Mohand was spared, as were the younger children. We were only at peace in the daytime, when father was out at work at the railway station.

But in the daytime I had to help mother, before and after school, or sometimes even during school hours. She was in the family way again. The fact that they were scarcely a happy couple did not alter the regular rhythm of pregnancies, which was only interrupted during my father's stay in Kabylia. My fate was the same as that of all the eldest daughters in the estate, on whom the mothers, worn out by successive childbearing, off-loaded their tasks. I helped with the washing-up, I learned how to make clothes and to iron; I did the washing in huge copper boilers, filled with water and laundry-soap. I had to be very careful not to scald myself, especially as I was very small, but I was used to it . . . I even washed the rugs, soaping them and then stamping on them to get rid of the dust, as we did in Kabylia. Then, my sister Fatima and I each took one end and we wrung them out, twisting them like plaits.

Like all the other 'big sisters' of the locality, I prepared the bottles, changed the nappies, burped all the children in

The Veil of Silence

the family. Our mothers brought the babies into the world and we brought them up. Seeing that you get attached in proportion to what you give, I loved my young brothers and sisters as if they were my own children. Moreover, I loved everyone, doubtless out of an unsatisfied need for affection. I reproached my father for his brutality, but I loved him all the same; I felt for some reason I could trust Mohand, in spite of his macho behaviour; I adored my mother, I couldn't believe she wasn't fond of me, I wanted to protect her, work for her later, get her out of that place. When I was scarcely thirteen, I was already mulling these plans over in my mind.

The most difficult time of the year was of course the month of Ramadan, when exhaustion was exacerbated by fasting. From the age of ten, I gradually trained myself to fast, first two days a week, Thursdays and Sundays when there was no school, then every day. Our parents remained faithful to the laws of Islam, as far as possible. My brothers were all circumcised, girls and women were dependent, but we ate pork, as in the canteen there was often no other meat, and never halal meat in any case. For my part, I had difficulty in finding our where I stood with regard to other religions. I had just had a short stay for observation in a sanatorium, in Cannes, for a minor health problem which required sunshine and rest. This sanatorium was run by Catholic nuns, whom my father had requested, in strong terms, to excuse me from any Christian practices. They agreed, but this didn't stop me hearing the other boarders reciting the Lord's Prayer and Hail Mary the whole day long, so that I too knew these prayers by heart. After that, before going to sleep at night, when I prayed for an improvement in our lives, I addressed myself sometimes to Allah, sometimes to

The Veil of Silence

Jesus. I have retained from these childhood relations with the next world a very strong spirituality, but a certain distance with regard to ritual and religious practices.

However, the one ritual that I was particularly fond of was the Feast of Aîd, forty days after the end of Ramadan, to celebrate Abraham's sacrifice: the sacrifice of the sheep. Possibly, at that time, it was the only gleam of light in our stormy sky. The women made cakes, there was singing and dancing, I saw my mother smile again, when she exchanged news from back home with her cousins, as they gossiped over the happenings on the estate, just as she used to at the well in Ifigha. My father was more relaxed that day, and more sober. We girls, who had scarcely left our childhood behind, spent weeks making new party frocks. I appreciated pretty clothes. An aunt who was a dressmaker helped to develop this coquetry, making my sister and me flounced frocks that were very fashionable at the time.

Even when it was not a holiday, I loved secretly dressing up. When my mother had gone out, I fell upon a box filled with scraps of material and secondhand clothes picked up at the fleamarket, and got myself up as well as I could. It didn't take much to make me happy: an old blue satin frock, sixteenth-century ruff, a former nobleman's costume all in rags, but with white lace and silky ribbons. I especially loved hats and shoes, long trains and veils. I played at being queen with my brothers and sisters, when mother had left me to look after them, then I would have to abandon the game to get on with my usual chores, as mother was very hard to please and was never satisfied with anything I did, no matter how much I tried and in spite of all my devotion.

I have to say that due to the life she led, her character grew daily harder. Nothing had changed with us. Oh, yes! Algeria was independent . . . We'd celebrated the liberation on 5 July 1962, in an atmosphere of incomparable

The Veil of Silence

jubilation. We were all dressed in green, white and red, the colours of the Algerian flag. Yuyus of rejoicing rang out on all sides in our temporary housing estate. In the space of one day, I found once more the festive mood of the great Kabyle celebrations of my childhood, then the usual suffering began again immediately afterwards. My parents' quarrels increased, becoming all the more frequent as my mother made absurd attempts at fighting back. I even think she'd tried to interrupt a pregnancy, unsuccessfully . . . Whatever she did, my father grabbed her by the hair, and dragged her round the floor. I would hurl myself between their legs to try to separate them, catching blows that he aimed at her. The next day, sitting in class, I relived these horrible scenes, and spent the whole recreation, sitting in a corner of the playground, crying.

However, at the Porte d'Ivry primary school I worked hard. I sang solo parts in the school choir, I got good marks for all subjects and my teachers set me up as an example to my school-fellows. I liked all my teachers, except possibly the one who taught history, because of a detail that I couldn't accept. She'd told us, in fact, how the French had stopped the Arabs at Poitiers in 732 AD, and had added, 'If it hadn't been for Charles the Hammer, thank goodness, we'd all be wearing veils today.'

I who rebelled against the submission and anonymity of women in our families, I ought to have been pleased with this witticism, but no: I felt hurt, certain that this woman considered us hereditary enemies, as we were descended from the invaders commanded by Abd al-Rahman.

In spite of this slight irritation, I shot ahead in history as in all the other subjects and reached the sixth class – the last class in the primary school – a year ahead of my age. Special permission had in fact to be obtained for me to be put up.

So, I would now be going to high school. I felt very

proud and rather relieved. The more I studied, the better chance I would have of escaping from the hell our home had now become. From now on, I was one of the big girls!

Alas! . . . For, as I grew up, I had reached puberty, and thus become suspect.

A girl, say the Kabyles, is a thorn in the foot, a stake driven into the back of her father and brothers. On the whole, a source of permanent anxiety and problems, necessitating a strict upbringing, for which the mother must be responsible, as, the older the child grows, the more things she is forbidden to do. If so many restrictions reduce her to tears, no-one will console her. She must learn to suffer, to be docile, to control herself.

First to control her body. To walk without running, wear long dresses covering her calves, gather up her skirts modestly to hide her legs when she sits down, and never sit facing a man. To hide her arms, too, and her hair, which is an object of desire: never loosen it or arrange it in front of a person of the opposite sex.

To control her high spirits as well as her appetite. To talk discreetly and eat with moderation, and above all never be the first to start eating at table. To curb any temptation to idleness: to learn all household tasks from childhood, to work in silence, to squat down when sweeping, moving backwards with her back to the men. Not to expect the slightest thanks for these tasks, however burdensome they may be but, on the contrary, to show herself grateful to

The Veil of Silence

her parents for thus teaching her her future job as woman and wife.

Above all, to control any urge to coquetry, sensual provocation, sexuality. To lower her eyes in front of boys, never smile at them, avoid speaking to them, stand aside to let them pass and always take a back seat. When her daughter reaches puberty, the mother explains to her that she is now in permanent danger from any male, and that her own feminine nature also constitutes a danger to her. The older she grows, the more she will have to fight against sentimental attractions and banish any physical excitement. She has been put into the world to marry someone chosen by her parents, and to give birth to children in her turn. If the chosen husband does not please her, she will not have the right to refuse him. To remain unmarried cannot be contemplated; a Chaouia[1] proverb states, 'For a girl, there is only marriage or the grave.' And she must be a virgin when she marries, on pain of being sent back by her husband to her parents who, thus dishonoured, must kill her, by strangling or poisoning or any other means.

How could I imagine, at thirteen and living in France, that I would be subject to this law to the bitter end – or almost? For these principles belonged after all to the patriarchal society of Kabylia. In Paris, these outmoded constraints seemed to have grown less severe. We did have to speak to men, if only to do our shopping or buy a bus ticket and, in the street, no girl would think of standing aside

[1] A Berber tribe inhabiting the Aures mountains. (Trans.)

The Veil of Silence

for every male passer-by, or to keep her eyes on her shoes whenever she met a man.

At home, however, I had to make myself small in front of my father and Mohand, who treated me with increasing suspicion. He was now seventeen and I was thirteen and a half. I was now an adolescent and I think that this metamorphosis upset him in some curious way; he felt it as a personal insult. He kept a jealous eye on me, forbidding me to go out, except to the lycée and back. He had no hesitation in hitting me when I came home late; he forbade me to play with my former gang and refused to let me wear fashionable clothes. Sometimes, in a sudden access of goodwill, he put on the kind big brother act, smiling when he spoke to me, bringing me a little present, taking me to the cinema, where I'd never have been able to go by myself. But if a boy just came near me, he went berserk, behaving like a primitive avenger, as if he felt responsible for all the virtue of Islam.

God only knows that my virtue was in no danger at that time! Not only was I too young to think of the slightest flirtation, but I had even sworn never to marry, forgetting that that too was forbidden. In my mind, all men were tyrants and I'd promised myself that after what I suffered with my father and Mohand, no other man would ever raise his hand to me.

Besides, I had plenty of more urgent things to think about than calf-love: sleepless nights spent in comforting the younger ones when my mother ran away to take refuge at a neighbour's; my father's brutality, when he then vented his alcoholic fury on me; all the various household chores; the lycée where I wanted to go on studying.

Only at school did I have time to compare the lot of girls from my country with that of French girls, who were less bullied, more open, freer. Even if, in those

The Veil of Silence

years, they hadn't yet started to kick over the traces when they left primary school, they were more respected than us, treated more like human beings. Compared with them, I felt diminished, a prisoner, mediaeval. Rebellion was brewing in me, as in nearly all my North African friends. I am aware, with hindsight, that we couldn't blame our parents who had themselves been brought up in the traditions they imposed on us. The ideal, for them, remained to settle their sons in a good trade, to marry their daughters in accordance with the ancient laws, then to finish their days in their own country, once their duty had been done. No doubt they were vaguely aware how fragile was their attachment to the past, no doubt they suffered from the fact that their former world was collapsing. Perhaps that might even have been the reason why my father felt helpless and sank into alcoholism: in any case, that is why I try to forgive him, now that he is no more . . . But we girls at the beginning of the sixties had more attractive models before our eyes than our parents, models which drew us like magnets. So we were preparing, without realizing it, for a conflict of cultures which was to cause many more victims than the French could then – or can now – imagine.

That being said, in spite of my taking Kahina-the-Rebel as my role model, at home I scarcely put a foot wrong, I was too afraid. I reserved my aggression for school.

'She's a born rebel!' said my French teacher.

I earned bad conduct marks all the time, except in Miss Filleul's English lessons, because, if I was born unruly, Miss Filleul must have been born with too little authority, and everyone took advantage of her. Her lessons were a general

The Veil of Silence

opportunity for playing the fool, no-one listened to her. So she needed to be defended. I rediscovered my spirit of leadership and imposed silence all round. Therefore, to reward me for my valuable assistance, she gave me full marks for conduct, which completely baffled the headmistress.

'You really are a mass of contradictions, Djura,' she said in amazement. 'You're a model of good behaviour in the lessons where everyone plays up and totally undisciplined when all the other girls are good as gold. Why?'

Why? Because I disliked both the injustice practised against Miss Filleul and the cane wielded too harshly by the strict teachers. Because I couldn't be obedient all the time, at home was enough. I needed to let off steam, to be provocative. Once, for example, the headmistress asked me what I wanted to do when I left school. With my head full of the lamentable and burlesque images of our fine 'emergency estate', I replied, as much ironically as insolently, 'I shall be a down-and-out!'

Beside herself with rage, she sent for my father and reported my behaviour.

'I don't understand,' my father replied. 'My daughter doesn't stir an inch at home. It's your job to see she's the same at school!'

Shortly afterwards, my friend Martine and I were expelled . . .

Martine was my accomplice, my confidante, as I was hers. For want of boys to talk to, I had a few best friends. Martine was French. She lived in a block of flats near the estate and often came to visit me at home, without telling her parents, who wouldn't have appreciated this association. I don't think she was very happy either. We soon became inseparable. We shared our troubles, and also our joys.

The Veil of Silence

Rather artificial joys, that we provoked by organizing fits of the giggles, laughing at the whole world. That resulted frequently in our being kept in detention, as well as other forms of punishment. It was no good the teachers separating us, putting one at the back of the class and the other in the front row, even with our backs to each other we found a way of exploding into uncontrollable fits of giggles. We were sent out of the room and we giggled all the more, although we knew we'd have to pay for the bad marks we earned, when we got home.

I also shared these light-hearted breaks with my friend Fanny, whose pretty mother had just died of cancer. As soon as our parents went out, we met in one or the other's house to play-act. Fatima, my younger sister, joined in. We put on *Doctor Cordelier*, a film that we'd seen on television, with Jean-Louis Barrault. This film had terrified us and we delighted in trying to recreate the atmosphere of horror. Fanny rigged herself out in a bowler hat, grabbed a stick and twisted her mouth to one side. We put out the light and Fanny struck three or four ominous sounding blows on the furniture with her stick, making us scream with terror. We switched on the light again, laughing like mad, then we started again, taking it in turns to play the part.

We danced a lot among ourselves to traditional or modern music. I often made up songs. Fanny dreamed of going into show business. She had somewhere or other dug out an 'impresario' who had made a vague promise to set her up. He'd given her a song – *The Four-leaf Clover* – that we had to rehearse for an audition. We got all worked up, but we were also rather mistrustful: it couldn't have been very serious and we dropped the matter. In any case our parents would never have allowed such eccentricity. Singers? Bringing shame on the family . . .

So then we had to be satisfied with imagining ourselves, like all kids from poor homes, in the shoes of the famous actresses of the day: Marilyn Monroe, Ava Gardner, Brigitte Bardot. These women fascinated me. I told myself that such magnificent creatures must surely be overwhelmingly happy. I was eventually persuaded of the contrary, when I learned that some of them had sunk into alcoholism and suicidal despair. I also understood, much later, that they sometimes conveyed a not very positive image of women, and that they too, in a different world from mine, were to some extent victims of a system. I am grateful to them, nevertheless, for having brought some light into my daily gloom, during those adolescent years, when my family picture grew daily darker.

And yet we had hoped for some improvement. In 1964 my parents had obtained a four-roomed flat in Courneuve, in the Quatre Mille housing estate, and my father had gone to be dried out. I was sure that our life was going to change.

Unfortunately, the anonymous atmosphere of the Courneuve rabbit-hutches turned out to be as depressing as the 'village' atmosphere of the 'emergency' housing estate. My father went back to his drinking habits. He was now on night shift with Renault, where they'd made no difficulty about taking him back. The war was over. He slept all day, insisting on everyone keeping quiet, which was hardly easy in view of the swarm of young kids who clung on to my mother's skirts, and on to mine. My brother Mohand had remained in the thirteenth *arrondissement*,

The Veil of Silence

with one of our maternal uncles, which didn't prevent him keeping an eye on me when I left the technical college where Martine and I landed up, after being expelled from the lycée.

I'd have preferred him to come and help me to face the fights between my parents, at least at the weekends. During the week, in fact, my father kept relatively quiet, given his working hours. But as soon as Saturday came round, his inner devil drove him to the local pubs, from where he returned home late at night, completely drunk.

Those nights I forced myself to stay awake, fearing his return. In the early part of the night I had recourse to reading, I recited poems, I listened to music, I told myself I'd get out of this, perhaps I'd get into show business one day, that I'd be free . . . Then, for long hours, I watched out for father's arrival, my nose glued to the window of my room on the thirteenth floor. In her own room, mother, too, was on her guard. As soon as we caught sight of father staggering along in the distance, we both slipped into bed, pretending to be asleep, hoping he'd respect our slumbers . . . But most often, he'd scarcely be inside, slamming the doors, than I'd hear mother screaming. Then I'd run and separate them, as always, except that now I was haunted by a new fear, that my father would hurl my mother out of the window, as he'd threatened to do several times, after a neighbour on the third floor had done just that to his wife.

As usual I got my share of blows, while my little brothers and sisters woke up crying, terrified. Mother fled to her cousins, or sometimes ran through the night, arriving at dawn at her brother's at the Porte d'Ivry. She stayed there the next day and I missed school again to look after the whole household while my father rested.

The Veil of Silence

Although I repeatedly promised myself I'd have a better future, there were times when I despaired. As Martine was also very depressed, we decided one day to commit suicide. The action of desperate youngsters, which could have ended tragically, but which turned into farce.

We collected indiscriminately every possible kind of tablets, sleeping-pills and others that we could find at home. When we got out of school, we swallowed the lot, equally indiscrimately, but not in any old spot! In the place d'Italie, near where we used to live, in a bar opposite the Hôpital de la Pitié. A predestined name which must have appealed to our subconscious. I think that in our innermost hearts we wanted to be saved and for someone to take pity on us.

We waited an hour, two hours, nearly three hours in this bar, and nothing happened! Not the slightest sign of discomfort. We began to go mad with anxiety. For dying was all right . . . Being saved, at a pinch . . . But to face our parents' anger at coming home so late, that was worse than anything!

Finally we made up our minds to go home, our eyes full of tears. Fortunately my father had already left for work and my mother somehow accepted some sort of explanation that I concocted. I didn't wait for anything more and went off to bed.

In the middle of the night I began to feel I was dying. I felt as though gongs were being struck in my head, my limbs were heavy and I groaned. I was in such a funk that I woke my sister Fatima who shared my room. I confessed my suicide attempt, but stopped her from telling my mother, who she wanted to call in her panic. Eventually she made me drink some milk. I learned later that this is not always recommended in cases of poisoning, but it worked with me; I got off with violent vomiting, and a fog in my head you could cut with a knife.

The Veil of Silence

During that misty night I dreamed I was gambling on triples, putting my money on 17, 3 and 1: in my dream that was the number of tablets of each 'make' that I had swallowed, counting them carefully. You can believe me or not, but the following day the Prix d'Amérique race was run and the three winning horses were, in the following order, 17–3–1. Naturally, I hadn't put any money on the race.

Nevertheless fortune, in a different guise, was to smile on me not long after. I had kept in close touch with my other best friend, Fanny. She had persisted in her wish for a career in the theatre or cinema, and had managed to get into the Jussieu Performing Arts School, in the rue du Cardinal-Lemoine. The performing arts! It didn't take me long to make up my mind: I also applied. Curiously enough, my parents didn't make any objection to my changing schools. I must admit that I cheated a bit. I simply said, 'I'd like to go to the same school as Fanny.'

Since his addiction to alcohol, my father had stopped taking an interest in my schooling, if not in my male associates. So, one school being the same as any other, he agreed. My sister Fatima joined us at Jussieu the following year.

Only this school was not the same as any other. It was everything I could wish for! The mornings were given over to general subjects and the afternoons to the arts: piano, dance and drama. If my parents could have suspected the attraction these subjects had for me, there's no doubt they'd have smelled a rat, but I took care not to let them into this sort of secret, and in any case I didn't have much occasion to unburden myself at home.

For my first exam in dramatic art, my teacher gave me the part of Antigone in Jean Anouilh's play. Antigone – the girl who says 'No' and challenges authority: the part suited me and I came second. As a matter of fact I should

The Veil of Silence

have been first, but I'd asked my friend Martine to feed me my lines, and naturally, as soon as the curtain went up, we burst out laughing. I had to begin the scene again, which meant losing marks. All the same, the jury congratulated me and I felt my wings sprouting.

I began to work like mad, with enough energy and to spare. The atmosphere at Jussieu represented a breath of freedom for me. I tried to compete with the other students in elegance. Because of my shortage of means I went in for eccentricity, the luxury of the impoverished. I dressed for comic effect, combining, for example, a grey pleated skirt and check jacket with a bowler hat, which one of my uncles had bought at the *Pélerins d'Emmaüs* charity shop.[1] I got up early to set my hair, trying to exchange my natural curls for Parisian ringlets. In fact I tried to make myself more European than I was. Not out of contempt for my origins but because, in the neighbourhood near the housing estate in the thirteenth *arrondissement*, I had had experience of the implicit racial prejudice towards 'Arabs': the archetypal knife-wielding Arab, the Arab woman with long fuzzy, henna-ed hair, the sly beggar-woman, possibly a thief . . . Even at the drama school, the teachers best disposed towards me told me I was too dark, that my type didn't fit the stock parts in the repertory, as if the whole theatre was blond.

So, every morning, I 'Parisianized' myself, curling my hair up to shorten it, with make-up in keeping. Then I hurried away before the others woke up, as it goes without saying I was forbidden to use any form of cosmetics.

I got on very well with my fellow-students. In between lessons we went off to the café next door to the school, to

[1] *Pélerins d'Emmaüs*, literally 'The Emmaüs Pilgrims', a religious charitable organization which collects second-hand furniture, clothing, etc. to distribute to the poor. (Trans.)

The Veil of Silence

talk for hours on end. This was our 'Young People's Club'. There was too much smoke there for me. I've always had a horror of nicotine addiction, but I've retained a taste for coffee which we drank throughout our endless conversations.

In the evening, before going home, I took care to wash my face in the toilets at the café, and then take off my stockings and bracelets in the lift of our tower-block, in Courneuve.

Sometimes my brother caught me in my make-up, as I came out of school, and then he terrorized me as usual. At other times, he pretended not to notice anything and took me to the cinema or an exhibition. He intended to become a photographer, and art brought us together. I was beginning to hope he might be able to persuade my father to let me take up the profession of my choice.

I was deluding myself: my father's reply was to be a veto, against which there was no appeal. When I was sixteen I was invited to play the main part in a TV series, *Pitchi and Poï*, which was going to be shot in various European countries. To travel, to star in a film! The gates of paradise were opening wide before me. The television crew offered my parents a nice round sum of money and also agreed to pay for a female chaperon, or for a male member of my family to accompany me.

My father's verdict fell like a guillotine: 'My daughter shall never go on the stage!'

I was in despair, realizing that obstacles would always be put in the path of my vocation as an artiste. For my father gave me unequivocally to understand that my age was not the sole reason for his refusal. In two or even four years time, it would be the same thing.

The Veil of Silence

I didn't give up for all that. I went back to the drama school, telling myself that I still had a lot to learn, and I must make the most of it. In any case, the lessons there were my only moments of happiness, and sometimes of enchantment. As part of our training we were sent as extras to the Buttes-Chaumont or Boulogne studios, where we also got to know something of the technical side of the profession. There, in the course of filming, I met established stars like Romy Schneider, Sophia Loren and even Elizabeth Taylor. I wasn't the type to go begging for autographs and I was too scared to speak to these sacred monsters, but just to see them from close to delighted me. One day, at the entrance to the studios, I bumped into Richard Burton as he was getting out of his green Rolls. He paused and said 'Sorry'. I realized how a seventeenth-century yokel would have felt if Louis XIV had apologized to him.

During my last year at the drama school, when I would be finishing my secondary education, I tried in vain to get round my father by suggesting alternative solutions. I wouldn't go on the stage, okay. But couldn't I perhaps go to the IDHEC[1] to train to be a film producer? Behind the camera I wouldn't show my face, I wouldn't make an exhibition of myself, I'd remain modest and discreet like daughters of Allah: my father could put his mind at rest. For my part, did not the cinema combine everything I loved: the sense of beauty, the sense of the text, music, poetry, sometimes dance?

It was quite hopeless: everything to do with 'art' disgusted my father and remained taboo, especially for a girl.

[1] IDHEC: Institut de Hautes Etudes Cinématographiques.

The Veil of Silence

The only thing he'd agree to was for me to study law. He'd always wanted one of his children to be a lawyer. My eldest brother had refused to go for this profession, and as I gave signs of being fairly gifted, he 'gave me my opportunity'. So, one day, he offered me the choice: 'You can either study law, or you stay at home like your fellow-countrywomen.'

I gave in, without much enthusiasm. I did the first year, aged seventeen, turning over in my mind the possibilities open to me. My plan was to continue with law, but the following year to register with a school of journalism to become an art critic. In this way, I could remain in a field which I liked. It would mean a great deal of work as, in addition to the Law School, I was working two days a week at the Prisunic in the Champs-Elysées to contribute to the family budget. My father insisted on checking my pay dockets and took everything I earned, down to the last penny. But it was all the same to me: I felt I had the strength to move mountains and I approached my eighteenth birthday with courage galvanized by my plans.

Then the sky fell in on me: forgetting my future as a lawyer, my father decided to marry me off.

To marry me Algerian style, without asking my opinion! He let me know that ever since I turned fifteen, he'd already been refusing numerous offers because of my schooling. But now he considered he'd waited long enough.

'If you don't marry this year, you'll never marry!' he yelled, obsessed like fathers from back home with the fear of having a misfit left on their hands.

Then he explained he'd given his word to a distant cousin he didn't even know, a man whose son had a good situation and wanted to marry me. The whole thing was stated as an irrevocable command.

The Veil of Silence

I was in a mad panic, determined to die – seriously this time – rather than comply with these barbaric transactions. After all, I wouldn't be the first North African girl to kill herself rather than accept a forced marriage. One day, a woman had done a broadcast on the Algerian radio about this. She had given girls who'd been forced into an engagement the opportunity to tell their story in a phone-in. It was dramatic. They telephoned from every corner of the land, saying, 'Tomorrow my father wants to marry me off, but don't count on it, I shall be dead before then.' They swore to take poison, to throw themselves into the sea, to . . . The broadcast had been interrupted immediately and the journalist sacked.

This incident had had no echo in France: it was believed here that such customs might persist in the depths of Algeria, but certainly not in France itself. However, this did take place in Paris as well: I'd just experienced this myself and I began to work out plans for a successful suicide this time.

Finally I decided that it was really too stupid after all to die simply because I wanted to live my own life. Wouldn't it be better to run away? That was easier said than done . . . Running away under these circumstances meant traditionally to bring shame on the family, to be discovered by one's father and killed by him, instead of doing oneself in.

Unless . . . Unless Mohand agreed to help me. Strange as it may seem, he was the only person who could come to my rescue as shortly before this he had married . . . my friend Martine!

For me, this had not been such a surprise when all's said and done. By dint of spying on me, my brother knew all my friends, especially Martine who was my invariable companion. He was attractive, a charmer, and, since Martine was French, he didn't have the same scruples

The Veil of Silence

he would have shown towards a girl from his own country. My friend found herself pregnant.

The affair caused a great to-do in both families but much less scandal in ours than if the 'dishonoured' virgin had been Algerian. Martine's parents, faced with a *fait accompli*, preferred to 'regularize the situation' rather than suffer the shame of an unmarried mother. As for my parents, Mohand had accustomed them to doing what he wanted since his childhood. He'd just turned twenty-one, he was of age and he could decide on his own fate.

However, no-one would agree to attend the wedding ceremony except me, absolutely delighted at the thought of Martine becoming my sister-in-law. That brought us even closer together. She and I were so fond of each other . . . Could I foresee that her very own daughter, Sabine, would come one day and kick my child in my belly?

Be that as it may, at the time, the precedent created by my brother might possibly turn out to be useful to me. It would be difficult for Mohand to refuse to be my ally, for all his moralizing. Besides, I wasn't asking him to be allowed to marry any Tom, Dick or Harry in defiance of my parents: I just begged him not to let me be married to a stranger. He was sufficiently emancipated, when all's said and done, to understand my attitude. Martine, for her part, was emphatic that he must plead with my father, which he did, without the slightest success.

Then the idea occurred to me to leave for Algiers with Mohand and my sister-in-law. In this way I could put a distance between myself and my father's anger. Moreover, I thought we might find interesting jobs over there. Algeria had just become independent; there was a need for young, enthusiastic professionals, prepared to

The Veil of Silence

build a new country, aimed at progress. At least, that's what I thought. We'd go and work in the capital, we'd find somewhere to live, and then we'd send for the rest of the family. Perhaps our parents would at last find some harmony again, once they were back in their homeland: I hadn't given up hope of seeing them reconciled. I was dreaming . . .

All three of us were dreaming, as Mohand and Martine soon fell in with my plan, but we kept our feet on terra ferma. To leave, we needed a minimum of money. We decided to take on extra jobs, at any hour of the day or night. My brother, proud of his new responsibilities, put our savings in a big glass jar. We ate as little as possible, we bought no clothes, our sole aim was to find a second-hand car so as to be on our way and be able to move around freely once we arrived in Algeria.

We put so much enthusiasm into this project that in a few months we had the necessary sum and the car. There remained the problem that I was not yet of age and my father fiercely opposed our departure.

When he wished, Mohand could be as shrewd as he was persistent: he called a family council, consisting of uncles and cousins who finally overcame my father's stubborn resistance, on condition that my brother stood guarantee for me, in the presence of witnesses. There again, I could not imagine what this transfer of powers would soon mean for me. For the moment, I was triumphant . . .

We left shortly afterwards, in January 1968, driving our old grey Peugeot 403 to Marseilles, where we embarked with the car for our homeland. I did not realize the irony of the situation: I was leaving France in the midst of the feminist revolution and just prior to the events of '68, to flee from the burden of ancestral Algerian traditions, and I was leaving for the Algeria of my

The Veil of Silence

ancestors to find freedom, as well as a more modern concept of life.

What is more, the ship that bore us towards the city of my hopes was called *'L'Avenir'* – 'The Future'. Was this not a good omen?

The crossing was pleasant, reconciling me with the sea. There were very few French people on the boat; most of the passengers were immigrants who had been expelled from France. The opposite, on the whole, of what I'd seen when I left Algeria in 1954, during a terrible storm and accompanied by a horde of Kabyles invited to work in the metropolis.

Martine and I were the only women on board. The crew were very friendly and allowed us to leave economy class and move into the tourist class with Mohand. Martine's baby, little Sabine, was not with us. My mother had agreed to look after her till we were properly settled on Algerian soil.

My brother was in a very good mood. The arrival in the Bay of Algiers was overwhelming: we were no longer used to such wide open spaces and such beauty.

After the usual formalities, we landed the car and drove straight into the streets of the white city, swarming with masses in white also: men in burnouses and many veiled women. Because he let his gaze wander, my brother jumped a red traffic light and a policeman stopped us. Mohand made the excuse of his excitement at returning to his own country: the policeman let us drive on. I'd have

The Veil of Silence

liked to get out of the car and stroll through the narrow alleyways which I didn't know. But the wish to see Ifigha, our native village – and for me, my impatience to embrace Setsi Fatima – was more important. We'd come back to Algiers later to look for work as planned.

The suburbs of the capital surprised me. Modern buildings had sprung up like mushrooms, buildings without style or charm. However, as soon as we got onto the narrow track winding along the coast, the magic of the scenery took over again.

We drove for a long time, in spite of our fatigue. After Tizi-Ouzou, I once more saw peasant-women dressed in multicoloured gowns working in the olive groves, wearing scarves on their heads, but with their faces uncovered. Then we started to climb, searching for Ifigha among the straggling villages clinging to the side of the mountain. Clearly we had no memory of the way. An old man directed us and finally we reached our native village, driving slowly along the rough road, escorted by a swarm of children. We stopped at the main square, as our house on the hilltop could only be reached on foot.

A crowd gathered round, firing questions at us from all sides.

'Where have you come from? From France? What! You're Fatima's grandchildren? Come, let's hurry and find her. Fate is smiling on her today!'

And they all set off to climb up the path with us. The women stared at Martine and me in amazement. I have to say that we were wearing trousers stuffed into high boots and blue cloth cloaks. My hair was frizzed in an Angela Davies Afro. This was the fashion in France at the time and we came from Paris. The village women, however, made no immediate comments on our get-up. They simply exclaimed, almost solemnly, 'So you are really Djura, Fatima's daughter . . . For you are her daughter, don't forget: she was the one who fed you, who gave you her milk, she is your mother.'

When we reached our house, I paused for a moment to get my breath, I was so excited at the idea of seeing my mother-grandmother again. Already the reality was different from my childhood memories: I'd thought everything was bigger, the square, the mosque, and now the entrance to our house that I'd imagined as enormous, and which was in fact a quite ordinary gate. What would Setsi Fatima be like?

She suddenly appeared, wearing a floral cotton *gandoura*, a headscarf tied on her forehead, her long henna-tinted plaits, hanging down her back. She had grown more gaunt, her face was heavily lined. When she drew back her thin lips in a smile, she showed she had only two teeth left, but she had retained her blue, limpid gaze which immediately drew tears of joy from me. She wept too, taking my head in her hands, then drawing back to gaze at me, clutching me tight again and murmuring between her sobs, 'My daughter, my daughter . . . Thank you for giving me back my daughter!'

Then she took her eyes off me to look at my brother and Martine. She said again, '*A revhiw, a revhiw!* What joy, what joy!'

And she took us indoors . . . I saw once more the whitewashed walls, the ancient beams, the striped woollen rugs of my childhood placed on a wooden chest that Setsi Fatima had painted herself. Soon I turned again towards the door which had been left wide open, to admire the Djurdjura Mountains and their eternal snows. I no longer heard the questions, nor the buzz of curiosity all around us. In my excitement I wondered why we had ever left here. In any case I had the euphoric feeling that a new life was opening up for me.

The Veil of Silence

In the evening Setsi Fatima installed Mohand and Martine in one of the little shacks round the patio. The building seemed pretty dilapidated and I swore to rebuild it later. Then I returned to 'our house', the one in which my grandmother and I had been so happy.

I examined it more carefully. In the cowshed there was no longer either cow or calf; Setsi Fatima had sold them a little time before our arrival as she needed the money. On the other hand she no longer slept on the ground but in a large iron bed which I was going to share with her. The mezzanine remained just as I remembered it, with its recesses for storage, its big jars of semolina, dried figs and lentils. The large room down below was also just as I remembered it, with the 'kitchen' corner and, in the middle of the room, the *kanoun*, the stove on which the galette was cooked over a wood fire and in front of which, in winter, Setsi Fatima, told me about Tseryl, the sorceress . . . I knew that all the fitting out of the interior had been done by my grandmother. But that was nothing exceptional: women were traditionally entrusted with this work.

There was still no running water or electricity. So, before going to bed, Setsi Fatima lit one of the oil-lamps that she made herself, with a wick fabricated out of strips of plaited rags.

'*Sekniyid taqejirtim!*', she said softly. 'Show me your little foot.' She had put the word 'foot' in the feminine, as she used to do when I was a baby, so recreating our former complicity.

Joining the deed to the word, she pulled off my boots, brought a basin of water and dipped my bare feet in it. Then she gazed long at them and stroked them, satisfied. Because 'little feet' are very important in the Kabyle notion of beauty. The traditional gown scarcely reaches the bottom of the calf, so the eye is naturally led to the ankles and feet. The smaller the latter are, the more the woman is appreciated . . .

The next day, the big question for Martine and me was: how were we going to dress? European or Algerian fashion? Then I remembered how my father had made it a point of honour – and of good manners – for my mother to land in France dressed like a French woman. So I opted for the *gandoura*, Martine likewise. My grandmother was delighted and brought out her finest outfits, kept for years in the hope of my return. We each put on a long embroidered gown, certain that our neighbours – male and female – would appreciate the gesture.

In fact, for days on end, they snooped and fussed around us – the women especially, for they were the only people to speak to us – and then the reproaches started. Out of pure whim, Martine and I had tied our red and gold *fouta* on the side, which brought down the village-women's thunder on our heads, and they forced us to tie them over our bellies, according to tradition.

Tradition . . . so the headscarf. The *amendil* camouflaging the sexual lure of the hair. In Paris, even if respect for certain customs remained obligatory with North African communities, girls didn't mind going bare-headed in the sixties. Here this was unthinkable. Only, just try to explain that to Martine who had never worn anything on her hair! As for me, the scarf was always slipping off my frizzy curls; my hair was far too short for me to keep the *amendil* on for long.

I explained our difficulties to Setsi Fatime who simply replied, '*Roulikem* . . . Well, never mind!' but her expression showed she was extremely vexed. Before long, moreover, she was pestered with reproaches on my account.

The Veil of Silence

'Don't let Djura walk about bare-headed like that,' the busybodies grumbled. 'People will take her for a whore. Her father didn't send her here for that. You'll be the laughing-stock of the village.'

Then I thought I'd found a solution. I asked Setsi Fatima to allow me to remain bare-headed at home if I promised I'd wear a hat when I went out. A hat hides the hair doesn't it?

That was the final horror! For, not to wear a headscarf is bad, but for a woman to wear a hat is simply diabolical! The hat is a symbol of virility, an exclusively masculine attribute. Why not a burnous, while we're about it! 'In any case,' mischief-makers recounted, 'they did in fact arrive in burnouses!' Oh yes . . . The loose cloaks we'd worn on the first day of our arrival, and which I'd thought so sensible, had been seen as an act of provocation on our part . . .

Then Fatima's women friends took my education in hand, not bothering so much about Martine, no doubt because she was French. They quickly forgave me my mistakes since I was so small when I left Ifigha. But from now on, I must conform to the local customs. First of all I was too thin, I had no hips: did we eat so badly in France? I had to fatten myself up . . . Also, I mustn't put kohl round my eyes, this was reserved for married women. Then, most important, I must not forget to lower my eyes when I met a man, and always stand aside to let him pass. I had heard of this duty in Paris, of course, but no-one respected it. Here it was compulsory.

At first, I was determined to conform to all these constraints out of common politeness, so as not to hurt Setsi Fatima, but also out of a sort of romantic idea of 'returning to my roots'. Martine, for her part, thought all this was exotic and rather fun at first, I imagine. After all, we weren't going to stay here very long. My brother was supposed to find us a place to live and jobs in Algiers. And, in the capital, even if you do meet some veiled women, you notice a good number of girls with their hair uncovered; they were no doubt more emancipated – at least, that's what I thought . . . Meanwhile, we conformed to the customs of the mountains where we were spending our holidays.

We even wanted to go to fetch water to help my grandmother who was exhausted by years of toil and the services she rendered to all the neighbourhood. In the morning she got up as early as before, then recited her prayers in Arabic, although she didn't understand a word of that language. Arabic had not succeeded in making inroads in our villages after all these centuries, any more than French after a hundred and thirty years of colonization, except in the case of the few inhabitants who'd had the chance of some schooling.

After her prayers, Setsi Fatima went off to fetch water. Only there were so many of us now, and more water was needed. Too much water! We didn't know how to economize as we should.

'In the desert, you can wash yourself all over in a glass of water!' Fatima explained.

I was heart-sore every time I saw her returning to the house, breathless, carrying her enormous jar full of water, on her poor old head. My sister-in-law and I could no longer bear this sight and one fine day we decided to go to the well ourselves.

We practised carrying jars on our heads, under the mocking gaze of the village women, and men who stood in front of the mosque, spying on us; it was no good, we couldn't manage this juggling feat . . . Then we each bought two aluminium buckets to carry. They were heavy, and to bring the equivalent of one jarful, we had to make several journeys. Some people thought us perfectly ridiculous: Parisian girls unable to adapt to Kabyle ways. Others thought we were doing our best

The Veil of Silence

to help my grandmother and that we were very brave to expose ourselves to mockery in this way.

Be that as it may, we remained objects of curiosity, creatures from the other side of the Mediterranean, 'free' girls. The village women came to examine this freedom, as they would have gone to gaze on extra-terrestials: with amazement but without feeling themselves directly concerned. The procession began early in the morning. They were there already, drinking coffee, while I was still asleep. Sometimes they brought bread, or figs. Those who had goats brought us milk and butter. Setsi Fatima received them with pleasure: she loved company. Even before our arrival, the women and girls were in the habit of meeting at her house: their husbands and brothers did not object, knowing there was no man there.

So, within a week, our house was filled with cakes, sugar and a hundred and one other delicacies. In itself, this was rather nice. But after the customary gifts, the visitors trailed after me, never leaving me alone for one minute. They examined me from every aspect. One day, one of them even came to feel my breasts, as if I wasn't made of the same stuff as her. The younger women seized on my bras, which I willingly let them have, or went into raptures over other articles of my underwear, while their elders renewed their various recommendations. Soon the children arrived, yelling or crying: I fled out of the house, keeping my eyes on the ground, it goes without saying.

There, I rediscovered the rapturous emotions of my childhood. The good Lord's narcissi spread their scent over the whole scene. I fastened them in my headscarf (I'd had to resign myself to wearing one) like the local girls did. I also picked enormous bunches of sweet-scented pink flowers that I put everywhere in the house, on the shelves, around the bed and even on the floor: I'd heard that flowers kept snakes away.

The Veil of Silence

A baby sparrow had in fact lead me to discover a nest of snakes in the mezzanine, at the sacrifice of its own life. I had just picked it up and as it was cheeping in my hands, I put it down on one of the shelves. It had immediately hopped behind one of the jars of corn . . . When I couldn't hear it any more, I tried to catch it again: a huge snake appeared instead, then slid away into a hole in the wall. It must have made one mouthful of the poor little sparrow! I screamed, to the amazement of my grandmother who was perfectly aware of the existence of this reptiles' nest. There's no doubt about it, my 'return to my roots' had many surprises in store for me.

Since then, afraid that these terrible creatures would emerge from their hiding-place, I filled the house with flowers to the general stupefaction, as here, flowers are intended to remain in the fields and not to serve as decoration. But I wanted to sleep in peace, to be at ease to read the poems of Omar Khayyam, to help with the sewing or peeling the vegetables – sitting on the floor, as is customary, without having to watch out in terror of these hateful creatures.

In the afternoons I resumed my childhood habits, accompanying my grandmother everywhere. We often went for walks in the countryside, visiting young women who had recently given birth, or to comfort sick women. Setsi Fatima showed me the land which belonged to my father. She pointed out each field by its name, explaining that, for her, selling a piece of land was like selling a piece of your own flesh.

We often went to a *douar*, which seemed to have been named after the tinkling of a bell: Tala-Gala . . . It was the ancestral home of my mother's family. In Tala-Gala,

The Veil of Silence

everyone was more of less related, and the atmosphere seemed less formal than in Ifigha.

The old women told me stories of the past, declaring that Si Moh or Mhand, the wandering poet, had stopped at the village. I listened to them, taking advantage of their chatter or their songs to familiarize myself with the Kabyle language, that my parents spoke at home it's true, but which I had lost the habit of using in Paris. My old 'cousins' in Tala-Gala, were delighted to see that I was interested in the culture of my roots. 'It's not like some girls, who wriggle their hips shamelessly, don't speak a word of their mother tongue and, just because they come from France, consider themselves too good for the rest of us!' They added, '*Tfou, tfou!*' and spat on the ground in disgust.

For some time, I thought that their sympathy towards me allowed them to take in what I said about 'emancipation'. I tried to make them aware of the fact that their society was made for men, their status as women only brought them forced labour, without any personal development to compensate.

'All that is quite true, my daughter,' they approved, showing me their arms which were nothing more than skin and bones.

'That's quite true,' they repeated, touching their wrinkled faces, their fingers bent and chapped from work in the house and the fields.

For two pins we'd have wept together over our respective fates. But for them, it was simply an established fact: they continued to accept their fate, even if they were beginning to criticize some of the practices which made my hair stand on end.

For example, a girl had recently disappeared. She'd been found at the bottom of a well. On enquiry, her own parents admitted having drowned her because she'd refused the

The Veil of Silence

husband they wanted to impose on her and what's more, they doubted her virginity.

'It's a scandal!' one of the old women exclaimed, but no-one spoke of forbidding these customs.

Another pregnant adolescent had tried in vain to bring on an abortion by using mysterious drugs and spells. When her mother and sister discovered her condition, they quite simply did away with her.

On hearing of these monstrous crimes, I congratulated myself on being brought up in France, far from these age-old brutal practices. I had after all been able to leave the house and to study, and I now felt myself in a position to choose my own future. The idea never crossed my mind for one moment that members of my own family, too, would one day burst in on me violently, and punish me for bearing the child of a man they had not chosen. Moreover, at this time, I persisted in the resolve I had made as a little girl: I had no desire to marry.

My single state perplexed all my confidantes, young and old.

'But why don't you get married?'

Friends of my own age, in Tala-Gala as in Ifigha, were waiting submissively for marriage. Some of them stayed at home, sharing in the domestic tasks, others were lucky enough to be able to continue their schooling – while preparing their trousseau, just the same. They proudly exhibited magnificent rugs which they had spent long evenings weaving. To make this cottage industry more attractive, several of them assisted in the work of one or other of the girls. In this way the weaving went faster and besides it was more fun. They called this mutual assistance 'lending their hands'.

They lent each other their hands, but did not dream of love. They simply prayed they would be offered a kind man, one who was understanding and gentle. They implored heaven, furthermore, not to give them too spiteful a mother-in-law. The supremacy of the mother-in-law remained an institution. If the daughter-in-law didn't please her and wasn't submissive, the husband's mother could pretty well force him to repudiate his wife.

I couldn't understand this obstinate determination on the part of 'mothers of boys' to perpetuate women's enslavement. Had they not themselves suffered under this yoke in the early years of their marriage! They ought to have broken the vicious circle by refusing to coerce and humiliate their daughters and daughters-in-law, when the time came. But no! According to the strangely wide-spread law of human behaviour, which requires the oppressed to take an inexplicable pleasure in becoming oppressors in their turn as soon as the opportunity arises, they continue to transmit the recipe for women's unhappiness, from generation to generation. *Mektoub*, it is fate.

I tried to persuade them that they could adopt new attitudes. That I for my part, refused to submit and to become part of this ridiculous system. I suggested that they unite, stubbornly refusing to be slaves, and escape from this endless cycle. I might as well be preaching in the wilderness . . . When I thought I'd found an embryonic female solidarity, I was in fact hitting up against a wall of resignation.

As for my own 'emancipation', I did not realize that it only existed in theory. The ancestral trap was not long in closing on me, and the facts were to make me face a reality that could hardly have been anticipated.

We'd been in Ifigha for several months already and I was beginning to grow impatient. My brother claimed he was still trying to find us work in Algiers, but he was sparing

The Veil of Silence

with his explanations. He didn't confide in Martine either. In fact he had changed completely since we arrived in Kabylia, and now modelled himself on the local 'lords and masters'.

He only spoke to us to give orders. He left for Algiers and returned without a word. When he stayed in Ifigha, he dressed in a burnous, went off shooting with his pals, then returned to one of the shacks round the patio, now set aside for him alone and his guests. My sister-in-law and I prepared food for these gentlemen which my grandmother took in to them, as we young women mustn't show ourselves to all these fellows. In any case, to tell the truth, I had no desire to associate with them. Tyrants like Mohand? One was enough for me.

For my brother had once again become as fault-finding as he was aggressive. He treated my grandmother like a servant and hit me for the least thing I did wrong, while no-one took any exception to his behaviour. *'Derguez!'*, he was a man and a man is always in the right. What is more, he took every opportunity of explaining that from now on I was under his guardianship, thus justifying his absolute authority over me. I was trapped . . .

For Martine, I suppose it was much more difficult. She had fallen in love with Mohand in Paris, they'd had a baby, but they had never lived together; she did not know his violence. Besides, in the euphoria of our departure for Algeria, had not Mohand said to us both, 'Don't worry about "customs". We come from France, we do. We shan't let them impose their old nonsense on us'.

How could my sister-in-law have imagined she would one day find herself ordered about, bullied, beaten by her husband? The first time my brother 'punished' her, she thought the world was falling apart.

'Algeria has completely unhinged him!' she said.

But Martine was less rebellious than me, and Mohand

The Veil of Silence

took advantage of this. Soon she was receiving double my ration of beatings. We consoled each other, giving way again to the nervous giggles of our schooldays, the only way we could break out of a sort of lethargy which gradually overcame us, for want of financial or legal means of escaping from this impasse.

One day, however, Mohand returned from Algiers with good news. He was accompanied by a French friend, Olivier, an architect he had known in Paris.

He took the trouble to introduce us, as Olivier had agreed to let us stay in a flat he owned in El-Biar, a very respectable part of Algiers. With all three of us on the spot, we'd have many more opportunities of looking for work.

A few days later, we packed our bags. I was delighted, and also vaguely uneasy. I'd had time to observe Olivier during his short stay in Ifigha, and I couldn't believe my eyes. So there did exist men like him, courteous, steady, full of consideration towards a woman? He looked at me a great deal and he seemed to like what he saw. I found that all the more agreable in that he himself was very attractive.

That being said, I had other plans in mind than to play the seductress. Although I didn't know Algiers, I had no sooner arrived than I made a list of telephone numbers of people who might be useful to me. I quickly found the possibility of resuming a course in dramatic art; I met a director of the RTA – Algerian Radio and Television – as well as several people prepared to help me. Offers came much faster than I expected. I was spoilt for choice as to where I would make my début, either in radio or television; to begin with, I was offered a job as an announcer or journalist.

Happy as anything when I came home from my last interview, I went off to tell my brother the news.

The Veil of Silence

'Out of the question!' he shouted. 'The RTA is no place for you! You'll never set foot there! Find something else.'

I'd escaped from my father to go from the frying pan into the fire! Mohand wanted Martine and me to work as shop-assistants at the Galeries Algériennes. I've nothing against shop-assistants, but really, I thought it ridiculous to have completed the studies I'd done in order to find myself behind a counter at the Galeries Algériennes, and once more my destiny was eluding me.

Fortunately, in the midst of all this, I unearthed two vacancies as clerks in the Mustapha Hospital for my sister-in-law and myself. This was preferable to the Galeries, and my brother didn't make much difficulty as it was better paid and we were broke. However, he stated categorically, 'You're not to have anything to do with your fellow-workers: you can soon get a bad reputation here. You don't have to chat with them, or even shake hands to greet them or say goodbye.'

He was speaking of men, of course . . . So we spent the day with our noses in our files, scarcely answering questions put to us by the male staff, convinced that our words and actions would be reported to Mohand.

The fact is that Algiers was still a village to some extent. Not everyone knew us, naturally, but they saw we'd come from France and spied on us all the more. We once again dressed in European style. It's true, we didn't wear mini-skirts, which were all the fashion in Paris at the time, but we dressed rather smartly and were quite pretty. Men stared at us in the street, which made Mohand furious. How dare these fellows look at us when we were with him! As for going out, except to the hospital, he forbade it more and more.

At home an icy atmosphere reigned, only broken by my brother's angry outbursts. Otherwise, not a word, not a smile, no communication in the presence of the master of

The Veil of Silence

the house. The only moments of relaxion occured when Martine and I were alone. Then we talked of our life in Paris, a life which had seemed so miserable that we'd tried to put an end to it, but now we agreed that those were the good old days. We bemoaned our fate together, saying in turn, 'Things can't get any worse.'

However, things were going to get much worse for me . . .

One afternoon, our friend Olivier came to visit us. My brother was not at home, but in any case Olivier was letting us stay in the flat, the least we could do was to offer him tea.

We were chatting merrily when Mohand arrived back unexpectedly. Was he annoyed to find us in good spirits? He turned pale. Without a word, he looked at me and pointed to the bathroom. I went in without quite knowing what he wanted. He followed me and shut the door. Then he slapped me hard across the face, grabbed me by the shoulder, dragged me into the passage, then out into the street where he forced me into his car.

'What's going on between you and Olivier?' he shouted.

'Nothing!'

The word was scarcely out of my mouth than another slap stung my face. I began to sob, swearing that nothing particular had happened.

'That man's got a thing about you!' my brother insisted.

I explained as calmly as possible that Olivier possibly did fancy me a bit, and that I, for my part, quite liked him.

Unwittingly, I had just signed my prison sentence.

That same evening, Mohand took me to Hussen Dey, a very poor working-class district, to a bedsitter that one of my maternal uncles no longer occupied. Was it so that

The Veil of Silence

Olivier would lose track of me? In fact, my brother's obsession went much further than just this one man: it was directed against all men. Mohand forbade me to take most of my dresses, which he considered too short, when in fact they came below my knees. I had to make do with the only skirt which seemed decent to him, and even then only after I'd unpicked the hem to lengthen it. This 'sensible' skirt was to be my undoing . . .

From now on, my brother came to fetch me every morning from my dilapidated building to take me to the hospital, with a skirt down to mid-calf as he wished. Only, this black silk skirt was soft and semi-transparent; I wore it with a pretty white blouse, quite plain, and patent-leather court-shoes. This made me look like a thirties vamp and the result of the operation turned out the exact opposite of what my brother intended: my unusual, attractive outfit now caught every eye.

When he realized this, Mohand lost his head. He made me leave the hospital for good, and shut me up in the bedsitter. I wasn't exactly locked in, but where could I go? Just to leave the building proved dangerous for a girl of my age. Hussen Dey was not a very safe neighbourhood, there were frequent muggings, rapes probably as well . . . Moreover, who could I ask for help when I knew practically no-one in Algiers? The police? I was still a minor, and under my brother's jurisdiction. So I remained for days in this squalid room, waiting for Mohand to bring me food, leftovers for the most part.

He prevented Martine from coming to see me, wishing to put an end to our relationship; we were too much in league for his liking. Sometimes he just brought me his daughter Sabine to mind. He'd recently sent for her from

The Veil of Silence

Paris, accompanied by a cousin. Martine was at work in the daytime, so the baby had to be looked after by neighbours or relatives during office hours. I was delighted to be one of these baby-sitters. I pampered the child, hoping she would not experience the same horrors as me, in spite of her tyrant of a father.

For myself I could see no solution. I was imprisoned, not for wanting to fall into dissolute ways, but simply to live up to my cultural aspirations. I had trusted my brother to help me realize my ambitions, and now here he was erecting a wall of prejudices and cruelty before me. As for Olivier, even if I had been in love with him, wasn't he a man like the rest? Never, up till then, had my brother warned me not to marry a Frenchman, or any other foreigner. Had he not himself chosen a French girl for a wife? Eventually I concluded that Mohand's reactions arose not only from the traditional autocracy of a brother, but also from a kind of excessive, jealous love.

Be that as it may, this imprisonment was to last for five months. Five months without exchanging a word with a single soul, without seeing another face except those of Sabine and her father, and that so infrequently! For hours on end, I gazed at the sea from the balcony of that single room . . . Several times I was tempted to throw myself out of the window and put an end to my suffering. But life seemed stronger, I wanted it to prevail, even though I often felt I was descending into a kind of madness.

Two records, miraculously left behind in the flat, helped me to overcome my despair and mental instability: Vivaldi's *Four Seasons* and Beethoven's Fifth Piano Concerto, *The Emperor*. I revelled in this music, making drawings on pieces of paper of the colours and movements which it inspired me with.

Except for listening to these records, the silence had become unbearable. I had no books to read. Then I

The Veil of Silence

began to compose poems and sing them, if only to hear the sound of a voice – my own. My vocation as composer-singer was born from this solitary confinement, above the Mediterranean horizon.

Sometimes I remembered that I was not only a solitary poet, but also a woman. I looked at my body in the mirror, in surprise. I'd forgotten I had a body. The body of a virgin, but with a mind so aged by suffering already . . .

At other times, I began to hope again . . . To hope for a miracle. I recalled the prediction made by a marabout my grandmother and I had gone to see a few months previously. A whole group of us surrounded the wise old man. He spoke briefly to each one of us, then gazed at me for a long time, saying, 'Do not worry. The planes will arrive this summer, and it will mean the end of your distress, to some small extent.'

The planes . . . Did that mean I would find myself one day on the other side of the Mediterranean, better treated than here? With this aim, I wrote letter after letter to my parents. I slipped out secretly to post them, trembling; I didn't really like going out in this neighbourhood. I begged my mother and father to come and find me . . .

I learned later how these letters had been received . . . My mother, in any case, had no more right to speak than before, the relationship between her and her husband had not improved – on the contrary. As for my father, he rejoiced.

'It serves her right! She wanted to leave, that'll teach her.'

He was delighted that my brother was making me suffer like this, and isolating me from indiscreet eyes. That proved he was playing his part properly and keeping a firm hold of me. I wrote to him again and again, asking him to sign a paper allowing me to travel and return home to Paris. He refused . . .

The Veil of Silence

One morning however, the door of the flat opened at a time when Mohand did not usually come. It was my father in person! I greeted him enthusiastically, overcome with gratitude, throwing myself into his arms: he had come after all to rescue me.

How could I be so naïve? He'd come for a holiday and wanted to see for himself how I was living. Not out of pity: just to check.

So we spent three days together, without saying very much to each other. Our relations had always been pretty silent and he was satisfied just to observe.

I was certain, in spite of everything, that this observation would make him feel sorry for me. No-one came to see me, I had no money, I ate scraps, I never went out, not to mention the danger of living in this unsavoury neighbourhood.

On the third day, he asked me thoughtfully, 'So you are completely alone here?'

There was an angry note in his voice. I thought, with some satisfaction, that he was certainly going to haul Mohand over the coals for abandoning me like this. I replied that of course I was alone; hadn't I told him so in all the letters I'd written?

He walked up and down for a moment without replying. No doubt he was going to feel sorry for me. I never stopped being optimistic, there's no doubt about it. For suddenly he burst out angrily, as if he'd made a discovery, 'So anyone can come and go here! Your brother's completely irresponsible! He doesn't keep an eye on you! You can even receive men!'

I was dumbfounded. So, far from pitying me, he was more or less suspecting me of being a prostitute, implicitly comparing the bedsitter to a brothel!

The next day, without further ado, he took me back with him to Ifigha . . .

The Veil of Silence

My brother took good care not to come and visit us there, having already suffered his father's anger in Algiers, on account of his 'lack of vigilance'! My father had it in for me, goodness knows why, and was not exactly gentle with me. Nevertheless, the stay in Ifigha had a good aspect. After long reflection, and deeming that I was not sufficiently supervised, he decided to take me back to France.

I could not control my impatience. The two weeks spent in the village seemed an eternity. I could not feel reassured until I was actually on the plane. Setsi Fatima had no need to question me to guess the trials I had endured. She knew as well as I did that the return to Paris, to be completely under my father's thumb, would not be a miracle cure.

'All the same, it's better for you,' she said when we finally left. 'Here you have no future. It's a country of jackals. Look what's become of you. You're terribly thin. A speck of dust . . . Just a twig. Come, my daughter, be brave, may God keep you.'

So I left her for a second time, fearing that it would be for ever.

The plane journey took place in silence. My father looked in one direction, me in the other . . . All in all, I felt a great sense of relief when I set foot in Orly.

My mother seemed pleased to see me, without however showing too much emotion. When her husband had gone back to work, she informed me that nothing had changed in the family situation: my father still drank and was as violent as ever. My brothers and sisters told me about May '68. My May '68 had been spent shut up in a bedsitter in Hussen Dey. And I still didn't know, on the evening of my arrival in Paris, that I had just moved from one prison to another. I never imagined that everything would be a bed of roses, but I thought at least I'd take up my former existence, look for a job and resume my studies.

The very next day my father settled matters.

'She'll stay here,' he told my mother. 'There's no question of her ever going out. Ever.'

I hadn't even the right to go to get the bread. I daren't slip out secretly: my father was still on night shift and stayed at home all day. He slept, it's true, but he might wake up at any moment. I spent twenty-four hours out of twenty-four on the thirteenth floor of our council-block in Courneuve, as much a prisoner as in Algiers; I had simply changed

The Veil of Silence

the view from the windows. Days followed days, months followed months. I helped my mother, I read myself stupid; fortunately books were not forbidden. I no longer had any heart for singing, I scarcely spoke. Sometimes I thought of Olivier, my handsome architect, who had doubtless forgotten me . . .

However, Olivier was moving heaven and earth to try to find me. He heard one day, from someone or other, that I'd returned to France. He was back in Paris himself and wrote to me immediately. Thank God I was the first to see the letter, so avoiding questions from my father.

I took my mother into my confidence, begging her to let me go and see him. If my father woke up, too bad; I would take the consequences.

So Olivier and I were able to meet surreptitiously for months. He had never imagined for one moment what I had gone through in Hussen Dey, nor what I was experiencing now in Paris. He proved infinitely considerate and patient, agreeing to our secret meetings, in cafés here or there, or more often in his car, not too far from my home, so that I could get back quickly. He also had to bow to my sense of propriety; our affair was totally platonic. Our ancestral principles had left their mark on me after all: you don't 'have relations' with a young man before you're married.

Marriage . . . Olivier was not against it, and the idea suddenly seemed brilliant to me: I was being offered a way out. If I were asked, even today, how much strategy and how much love went into my intention to get married, I'd be incapable of replying. I was in love with Olivier, under the spell of, 'his decent behaviour, his affection. But all the same, I'd been a prisoner for more than a year and a half; it's not surprising that my main desire was to escape, by whatever means. And, not only did this way seem the most attractive, but it was the only way.

The Veil of Silence

I talked to my mother about this plan, asking for her advice. What should I do?

'He's French,' she remarked . . .

'Yes,' I replied, but he's a friend of Mohand's, 'he comes from a humble but respectable family, he's an architect, and besides papa has never said I shouldn't marry a Frenchman.'

'We can always try,' mother sighed. 'Let the young man come and ask for your hand . . .'

To my great surprise, my father proved almost affable.

'Listen, young man, I've nothing against your marrying my daughter, only we are two brothers and we are accustomed to making this kind of decision together. So, if you don't mind, you'll have to ask Djura's uncle for his permission.'

So Olivier takes the plane again, for the uncle lives in Kabylia!

'You know, our society is now advanced,' my uncle decides. 'If Djura and my brother are in agreement, well . . . so am I.'

Olivier immediately sent my father a letter . . . which my mother and I hurriedly steamed open, in our impatience to know the verdict. We were so delighted that we circulated this message of good cheer round the whole family. After which, we re-sealed the envelope and took it to my father.

He went off to read it in his room and made no comment. Not a word, nothing! He acted as if this epistle had not come from Olivier, as if he had never received his letter. He simply proved doubly suspicious of me, spying on me day and night.

Then I realized that he'd led me up the garden path,

The Veil of Silence

that he'd made a fool of Olivier, that he'd never agree to my marrying a Frenchman, that I was cloistered for good; I decided to run away.

To run away, with all the risk that it entailed. My father, 'dishonoured', would certainly decide to do away with me. I would soon be of age, it's true, in the eyes of the law – but not according to 'our' laws. I was an Algerian woman, so an eternal minor. But I was prepared for anything, rather than continue to live like this.

I revealed my plan to my mother, with the secret hope that she would be able to defend me from my father, when the time came.

'You know, I'm not leaving to run after a young man, I'm going so I can live an independent life. I shall go to a girlfriend's to begin with . . .'

This was true. A former friend from the Performing Arts School, who I'd managed to contact secretly, agreed to come and fetch me in her car one night . . .

My mother, up to now in league with me, then barred my way, hit me in an attempt to stop me leaving. I suppose she was afraid of reprisals from my father.

She was right. When he came home the next morning and realized I'd gone, he took a revolver and went off like a madman, yelling, 'I'll kill her, I'll kill her!' Then, not knowing where to find me, he went back to take it out on his wife, accusing her of having brought me up badly, and punishing her for this error.

I learned these details when I saw my mother and my sister Fatima again in secret, from time to time, in a café or a doorway. By then I had found a job as receptionist and, at the same time, resumed lectures at the University of Vincennes, in the Department of Cinematography. I found accommodation in a servant's room, to Olivier's great astonishment. He repeatedly said, 'Why don't you

The Veil of Silence

come and live with us? My parents are very fond of you, and they're ready to welcome you.'

In fact his parents were adorable and quite disposed to adopt me. But I was still bogged down in my old principles, in spite of my permanent rebellion, and didn't want it to be said that I'd 'gone off with a man'. I wanted to prove to my parents that I'd remained a girl with a 'sense of honour.'

This obsession spoilt my first night of love with my 'fiancé'. Honour or no honour, I couldn't go on refusing myself to this man. So, one night I agreed to sleep with him, at his parents' home.

I thought myself emancipated: I approached this intimacy burdened by all the taboos. I was going to lose my virginity outside the bonds of marriage.

I can imagine to what extent this reaction may seem anachronistic, but that was the way it was. The symbolic implications of virginity pursue a girl in our society as soon as she reaches puberty. The morning after the wedding night, the sheets stained with the virgin's blood are exhibited at the window, as proof of the new bride's virtue, for all to see. As for being guilty of sexual acts before the nuptial ceremony, it had been sufficiently explained to me, in Ifigha, that for this the ultimate penalty was sanctioned, even if the girl had been raped!

I recalled all these practices, unconsciously, but it was not really that which made me unhappy: it was that, from now on, I could never prove to my father that I had remained 'a good girl', and that he ought to have trusted me.

I was all the more confused in that Olivier did not attach any real importance to this mark of good behaviour, so preciously guarded.

That being said, it did not take me long to blossom in the field of the senses. If anything could have inhibited me, it would simply have been violence. I would never have felt at ease in the arms of a man like my father, or

The Veil of Silence

my brother, or so many other husbands: torturing you by day, and making children for you by night. But Olivier was a most gentle companion, kind, considerate, and very much in love. For nearly five years he had plenty of time to tame me . . .

For the whole of 1970 I was ridden with anxiety. The fear of meeting my father never left me. I imagined I could see him everywhere, I turned round at every moment in the street, starting as soon as I heard the slightest footstep outside the door of my room.

I met my mother more and more frequently, late in the evening. I gave her most of my earnings, to help her save. Had my flight put ideas into her head? She too was thinking of leaving home with the children, or some of them at least. In my frantic desire to liberate everyone, I promised to take care of her when she was ready . . .

'For the time being, be careful,' she said. 'Your father is looking for you, he's armed.'

This daily terror eventually became unbearable. I was not going to live all my life like a condemned person on the run! One morning I summoned up all my courage and decided to stake everything – neck or nothing – in other words, to confront my father.

I went to the Gare du Nord, where he caught the train back to Courneuve, early in the morning. When I got to the concourse, I nearly gave up, I was in such a panic. But I couldn't believe he would shoot me, just like that in public. So I went to stand at the top of the stairs, where I was sure not to miss him. Soon I caught sight of him in the distance, carrying his satchel, looking grim and preoccupied. I felt the blood draining out of my body, my hands were sweating, I could scarcely breathe.

The Veil of Silence

When he saw me he didn't seem surprised. You'd have thought he was expecting me. No revolver, no slaps. I almost embraced him, but I didn't dare.

'Good-morning, papa . . .'

He smiled slightly and took my arm as if to pull me on to the platform.

'Come home!'

His tone was threatening. So, he hadn't understood anything. He simply thought I'd come to ask his forgiveness before returning to the fold. I drew myself up to my full height and asked him bravely, 'It seems you want to kill me?'

'Come!' he insisted, pushing me slightly.

'I can't come with you now,' I said, 'I've a class in an hour. But we can go and talk in a café.'

He remained dumbfounded for a moment. To go with him, my father, to a café, traditionally out of bounds for girls! He agreed, nevertheless, still convinced that, if I was there, it was because I had given in.

So there we were, in the boulevard Magenta, sitting in a pub with red leatherette benches, me asking for news of my brothers and sisters, my mother, my family . . .

'Things are okay,' he grunted, 'but you know it's your mother and your uncles who are urging me to do you in. If you come home, nothing will happen to you.'

He pronounced this promise of clemency, accompanied by a very clear threat, with a triumphant air, delighted to have his prey at his mercy.

Then I decided, once and for all, that we could never come to any understanding. Firstly, because he was lying: my mother and uncles had never encouraged him in his need for vengeance. Then, because I felt that nothing would make him change his mind: I was to return – stay at home, period.

Then I too lied. I promised to come back to Courneuve

The Veil of Silence

the next day. I got up, kissed him on both cheeks and said, 'See you soon, papa.'

I did not see him till sixteen and a half years later – on his deathbed.

Shortly afterwards my parents separated. Or rather, my mother did a midnight flit, like me, with five of her children. The flat that Olivier and I found for her proved too small for eight people, so we agreed that Fatima and Belaîd, aged twenty and seventeen, would remain in Courneuve and leave later. Fatima could manage my father, and as for Belaîd, he was a boy, and would have no problems.

We hurriedly loaded clothes and schoolbooks into a van rented by Olivier, and drove off like burglars.

My mother had never had a job all her life, and in any case the children she took with her, aged from four to thirteen, demanded all her attention. She could have done some cleaning, but she didn't want to. I hoped to spare her, to console her for all the suffering she had endured. So I became the head of the family . . .

I worked like mad, at the office and at home. I had set as my aim to take charge of my brothers and sisters until they were of age, and to look after my mother to the end of her days. I did not quite realize what a burden this decision would be on my young shoulders. I paid the rent of the flat, which we had taken in Olivier's name, as a brood of Arab children with an illiterate unemployed mother didn't inspire anyone with confidence. I went in the early morning to the wholesale markets, to save on the cost of food, I bought clothes at the sales, which my mother altered to fit each child in turn.

I also had to be responsible for the little ones' schooling

The Veil of Silence

and their psychological development. My mother, happy to have escaped from the marital yoke, proved nevertheless incapable of doing anything about her children's education and training them for normal life. I became a surrogate mother for her progeny, in addition to being a substitute father.

It was not easy. Amar, one of my young brothers, was a great worry to me. Already, in Courneuve, he'd been associating with young delinquents, which resulted in interference with his schooling. He continued to get up to mischief. Several times I had to go to retrieve him from the police-station for stealing umbrellas or other trifles. Then he began to play truant, and was expelled from school. At the sight of his weekly reports, no state school would accept him. I had to pay for him to go to a private school which left me completely broke.

My sister Malha was in perpetual revolt against my mother. Hakim and Djamel, and even Djamila, the baby, suffered from the after-effects of a childhood spent in the streets of the Quatre-Mille housing estate, with an alcoholic father and a mother beaten stupid.

Nevertheless I still had hopes of turning them into mature human beings, capable of some satisfying occupation. I would find nothing impossible, providing I had my health and strength.

Well, I was strong as a horse, but a sloppy sentimentalist at heart. Nothing had changed in me since I was fourteen. I adored my brothers and sisters, as if they were my own children. I trembled as soon as one of them fell ill, no exertion was too much for me. My mother cleverly bolstered up my courage.

'With Djura,' she said, 'it's as if I had ten men!'

That's all I needed to make an extra effort. I was sure I had finally won the love of the mother who had refused me her milk. I had the occasion, subsequently, to realize that

The Veil of Silence

this fine delayed-action show of love was nothing more than her appreciation of comfort.

The only genuine love I could boast of was Olivier's. He made an effort to understand the situation, boosted my morale, and willy-nilly accepted the family folklore. He stood security for successive flats, without ever grumbling. For we frequently moved house. We still had my father on our heels, more determined than ever to make my mother and me pay for our escape. My mother's family warned us when he picked up the trail and we decamped again, driven by my boyfriend (not yet become my husband). My mother didn't want us to marry. Was she afraid of what people would say?

'You see,' she explained, 'if you get married now, people will be convinced I've given you permission to marry a Frenchman since I've left my husband.'

A Frenchman... She didn't even realize her own racism, nor the implicit insult to Olivier who helped me more than once to make ends meet, although he didn't earn a fortune from his job in an architect's office.

The only thing she accepted, after a certain time, was for Olivier and me to live together. 'As long as no-one knows . . .' So first we went to live with his parents, then in a tiny flat, while still being responsible for my mother's flat and her whole household.

In the midst of all this, my brother returned to remonstrate with my parents and try to reconcile them. I took good care not to ask him to my place and no-one let him have my address. I met him at mother's flat. He took the opportunity of beating the living daylights out of me.

My parents set up together again for three months, and the carnage resumed. Re-removal, with me called on to help again, me resuming responsibility for bringing up the kids and everything . . . Only this time my mother wanted a divorce. My father had just lost his job so had much more time for drinking. His state of almost permanent intoxication made him more or less indifferent, so that he was less determined to try to find us, although he continued to threaten us.

The bright spot in all this was the University of Vincennes, which I found time to attend in the evenings with Olivier. Besides his activities as an architect, Olivier shared my interest in the cinema. Vincennes, at this time, was in the midst of revolution. I took part in the fights against racism, for more social equality and for improvement in women's condition. I was not a member of any political party, but I fought for justice and liberty everywhere.

We were lucky to have outstanding teachers, like Gilles Deleuze and Jean-François Lyotard who became our gurus. In the cinema world, things were on the move also. Olivier and I attended the same courses. It was wonderful to share the same passion, the same ambitions, the same hopes.

We planned to collaborate over a photographic report on the use of colour in Algerian architecture. Our aim was to show that this so-called primitive architecture had eventually influenced artists as ultra-modern as Le Corbusier. In order to succeed in such a vast enterprise, we would naturally have to travel through the whole of Algeria and collect sufficient material for a short documentary, then transfer our various photographs on to film. We decided that this would be how we'd spent our holidays.

The Veil of Silence

Dangerous holidays, obviously, as my eldest brother was still in Algiers. Could we escape his clutches?

Olivier was of the opinion that the best thing would be to confront him. As I could not get off from my work until a month after his own leave began, he wanted to set off to see how the land lay . . . convinced that he would be able to renew reasonable relations with my brother. Mohand had become a photographer. He was even preparing a book on the interior of Kabyle houses. Perhaps the similarity of our aims would bring us together? Olivier took his equipment, his ancient Peugeot 404 and set out . . .

His first visit was to Mohand, who welcomed him with open arms, surprised that I was not with him.

Olivier wrote to me immediately to allay my fears. Mohand apparently now considered our 'liaison' as official. Time had passed, he was no longer angry with me. He even put Olivier up in the bedsitter in Hussen Dey, of sad memory, but which he had since converted into a photographic laboratory.

I couldn't believe the letters from my dear traveller: I was going to find an amicable brother, as well as see my friend Martine again. Olivier and I were going to succeed in our first documentary and try a new experiment in this Algeria which was still so dear to my heart.

My brother and Olivier came to meet me at the airport. I looked first to see Mohand's expression. He smiled broadly at me, and this made me forget my past grievances.

We kissed and Mohand took us to dine at his flat. There

The Veil of Silence

I saw Martine again and my maternal uncle, who lived in Algiers and who I was very fond of. He had to go to meet his sister at the airport later in the evening. She was also arriving from Paris, and as she could not travel on to Kabylia the same evening, it had been agreed that she should spend the night at my brother's and we would sleep in the bedsitter in Hussen Dey, where Olivier was already installed.

'Can you drive my uncle to the airport?' Mohand asked Olivier after dinner. You can drop Djura and me in Hussen Dey and I'll take the opportunity to show her the photography lab. We'll wait for you there, and then you can give uncle, aunt and me a lift back here. Okay?'

So we all left together in Olivier's car. It was a delightful drive through Algiers on this fine summer evening. My brother pointed out various districts to us, commenting on his projected book on Kabyle houses, asking about our own impressions of the local architecture. I felt happy, freed from all my former tensions.

However, when Mohand and I got out of the car at the entrance to the Hussen Dey building, and I saw my uncle and Olivier drive away, I felt a prey to a spasm of misgiving. Was it the memory of those painful months spent here? Or the persistent fears that I still subconsciously felt in my brother's presence? Yet nothing justified that sense of apprehension. All the same, my disquiet increased so much that as we were climbing the stairs I nearly turned and ran.

Too late . . . Mohand has already opened the door of the flat; he shuts it behind us, pulls a knife out of his pocket and states coldly, 'Now, you're going to die.'

Before I have time to utter a word, he throws me onto the bed and sets about punching and slapping me as hard as he can, nearly breaking my nose. My white blouse and sky-blue skirt are soon covered with blood. I mop my face with my white scarf which also turns red. I stammer, 'But you welcomed Olivier, you knew how things were. You told him that . . .'

More blows immediately silence me. Now Mohand is sitting near me on the bed, fingering his knife, savouring my terror.

'You love this fellow? Well, you're going to die because of him . . .'

It's crazy, but my first thought was for my mother. What would become of her, with no resources, humiliated by the fact that her daughter had been murdered by her own son?

Then, in a sort of fog, I glimpsed the extent of my naîvety. I would never escape! However much I worked, however much love I lavished on them all I always came back to square one: my father and my brother, two men who wished me dead. What else did they want in fact, except my death? The impossible . . . That I should get married, but not to a foreigner. That I work, but hand over my earnings to them, without enjoying the slightest freedom. That I refrain from making any decisions and, most important of all, that I do not dispose of my own body.

Mohand produced photographs that Olivier had taken of me, in a very low-cut dress, and waved them about like a madman. 'For that, too, you're going to die!'

He'd gone through my boyfriend's things. He'd foreseen everything, prepared everything. And I'd fallen into the trap once more! I have to say that as far as double-dealing was concerned, he had surpassed himself this time. I had delivered myself up to him with a smile, and now I was sobbing bitterly, no longer tears of anger, nor even of pain, but tears of despair, of extreme exhaustion, of humiliation. I no longer even tried to argue, I listened to my brother ranting and raving without hearing a word, I no longer

The Veil of Silence

looked at him, preferring not to see when and where the knife would strike. I let him exult over my terror, my resignation, my downfall . . .

Then I tried once more to justify myself, without any illusions, but with the idea of spinning things out, gaining time, until the others came back.

But no-one came. I heard later that my aunt had missed her plane, my uncle and Olivier had waited for a second flight, then telephoned Paris to learn eventually that she'd leave another day . . . And all this time, I lived through an eternity of agony . . .

Suddenly I heard footsteps in the passage. I leapt towards the door. Mohand held me back viciously, with this ridiculous expression, 'Not a word of all this!'

However, there was no need to say anything: I was an edifying sight . . . My uncle showed no real surprise: a brother who punishes his sister and lays into her till her nose bleeds is not so exceptional in our world. Olivier, for his part, was stunned. He admitted to me later that he hadn't dared do anything, waiting for me to make some move. But my brother didn't leave us time for any explanations.

'Okay, let's go,' he said with an innocent smile.

And he pulled me by the arm, requesting Olivier politely to give him and my uncle a lift back.

The journey took place in heavy silence. Olivier drove, with my uncle beside him, Mohand and me sitting in the back. He first dropped my uncle, who didn't linger over his goodbyes, then Oliver stopped the car in front of Mohand's block, expecting him to take his leave also.

But Mohand opens the door on my side, shouting, 'Get out, you, get inside where you belong!'

The Veil of Silence

My father . . . The same words as my father, a few months earlier. The same prospect: four walls, held captive by force, silence, shut away, fear . . .

Without thinking I begin to scream, 'No, I won't get out!'

Then Mohand brandishes his knife again and slashes my lower lip. I open the door and run away with my brother after me, trying to catch me. We run round the car, Olivier attempting to get between us.

'Don't you move, you!' my brother shouts. 'You've deflowered my sister, this slut, this trollop!'

He calls us all sorts of names. Olivier does what he can, but he's no karate black-belt, and we aren't in a film. I defend myself like a fury.

'No! I won't go home with you! I'll call the police!'

As if the police could save me, in a country where a girl who rebels is automatically considered guilty.

The caretaker of the building, alarmed by the noise, then appears on the scene.

'She's my sister,' my brother indicates simply.

And that is more than enough! Without worrying about the reasons for our quarrel, nor the bloodstains on my clothes, the caretaker grabs my shoulder and starts yelling too, 'Okay! get inside, you!'

Definitely, that seems to be the only thing the men round here can find to say. I struggle with this multi-purpose caretaker who tries to prevent me getting back into the car. But my brother suddenly gestures to him to stop. Has my threat to call the police had an effect after all?

'Let them go,' Mohand says. 'In any case, I'll find them again.'

Then, turning to me, he adds, 'You hear? Wherever you are, wherever you go, even if it's to America, even if it takes ten years or more, I'll find you and kill you.'

The Veil of Silence

Olivier puts his foot down and drives off like the wind . . .

A few miles further on, Olivier stopped the car and took me in his arms; we had not exchanged a single word.

'You're sorry you ever met me, aren't you,' he said most sadly.

I shook my head through my tears. 'No. I probably chose the difficult way, that's all.'

We drove full speed to the bedsitter to pick up the photographic equipment. When we got there, I changed, washed my face and fixed a plaster on my lip which was still bleeding. My eyes were swollen, I had a split lip and a cauliflower nose: I was disfigured.

We spread a large sheet on the ground and bundled up all our things in it: cameras, documents and clothes. Then without delay we did a midnight flit. I was going to say: as usual . . .

We drove for a long time without speaking, then Olivier said, 'Would you like us to go back to France?'

In a daze, I replied, 'Yes.' Olivier stopped the car, we were both exhausted. We slept for several hours, by the side of the road.

I awoke as if from a nightmare. Only it wasn't a nightmare: the proofs were there, before my eyes. The sheet in which all our possessions were bundled, my swollen face, covered with bruises, unrecognizable. Why was fate so much against me? I had everything: youth, health, beauty, courage, enthusiasm. I only asked for the right to drive

The Veil of Silence

around, admire the scenery, take my little pictures, bring off my first piece of creative work in honour of Algeria. Was all that to prove impossible?

Well, no! Definitely not! Whatever may have occurred, I was not giving in. I was an Aries, and as a Ram I would continue to batter. We'd had an enormous job to collect the necessary funds for this trip, to obtain permission to photograph or film, and were we about to abandon everything because one single person – my brother – was opposed to our venture?

'We won't go back to France,' I announced to my companion. 'We're not going home empty-handed, just like that, with blank films. We're going on.'

Olivier smiled, kissed me affectionately and started up our good old Peugeot.

To say my country is beautiful is an understatement . . . I discovered it, entranced, from the Jijel Coast to the south, through Bougie, Collo, la Calle. Our itinerary took us through Bou Saäda, Biskra, the seven cities of Mzab, the desert, El-Oued, Touggourt.

We drove and filmed as fast as possible, certain that my brother was on our track. Naturally we had avoided Kabylia and I had to give up the idea of going to embrace Setsi Fatima: we were sure to be caught in Ifigha. But we saw other wonders of architecture and scenery. We slept in the open, which is very pleasant in August, except for several attacks or attempted thefts from which we escaped fairly lightly. I must say, we'd experienced worse . . .

The villages were hospitable. The people sometimes seemed intrigued to see me in the company of a foreigner. One day, a good fellow asked me, 'Tell me, are you his lady?'

The Veil of Silence

We dodged awkward questions by talking about our work. We carried our cameras hung round our necks to make us look like reporters. The inhabitants of our land don't much like being photographed, especially in rural areas. But as our targets were mostly objects, they left us alone. So we got our supply of old houses, shop-windows, decorated doorways, wells, mosques, each one more magnificent than the last. We ate as the fancy took us, here a cake, there a dish of semolina. I can still taste the fritters with honey that we sampled in the Casbah of Constantine. And the lemon ices, a speciality of Collo, one of the most beautiful towns in Algeria, where the mountain drops down sheer into the sea.

In El-Oued, we could admire the land of the thousand domes which seem to rise out of the ground like so many statues. The desert stretched out at our feet.

The desert . . . Endless miles, a mixture of the end of the world and the promise of eternity. A reflection of my own moods? No matter what raptures I experienced in this magical land, I dragged around with me everywhere the feeling of an irreparable break, the burden of a point of no return, when things have gone too far. No reconciliation would now be possible between Mohand and myself. But why had he done this? Then I thought of my father, also banished from my own existence – through his own obstinacy. God knows that I had showed bursts of affection towards both of them, without moving them for for one moment. Were they denuded of all sentiment? Did paternal or brotherly love remain a dead letter to them?

Then I watched this vast expanse of desert roll by, monotonous, boring and yet magnificent, inspiring respect, serenity. I told myself that the answer to all these questions – let's say the solution to all my problems – was perhaps there: in the poetry of things and the road we were following. I found myself faced with a choice, as if I were

The Veil of Silence

gazing at the two pans of a scale. On the one side, the pan weighed down with hatred, jealousy, baseness and ancestral conflicts; on the other, the pan of wisdom, receptiveness to others, generosity, peace. For me, the scales tipped towards this side. I gazed at Olivier fondly. He looked happy and terribly tired.

The fact is, we were pressing on very fast. In spite of our excitement at our discoveries and the enthusiasm we put into our creative work, we were feeling the exhaustion of a race against the clock. We were afraid of being followed. It was beautiful, magnificent, sublime, okay! But the faster we got home, the faster we'd be out of danger. At least, imminent danger. We would put the sea between Mohand and ourselves. I tried to forget his last threat that made light of all frontiers and even oceans.

We arrived in Paris knackered and with me in a pitiful state. My lip was gradually healing, but I had developed some allergies as a result of the shock my brother had inflicted on me. My whole body was covered in a rash and I itched down to my finger tips. We called a doctor who examined us both and, to crown everything, announced the great news: 'You've caught scabies. But don't worry. It will have cleared up in a couple of days.'

I looked down and began to laugh as I hadn't laughed for ages.

'Now we must edit the film,' Olivier said gently.

So I set to work again, cured of my scabies, but not of my fear. Fear to which I was a prey every moment, fear which was not to leave me for years, fear which from now on was part of me. Mohand's words remained imprinted on my mind. 'Wherever you are, even if it takes ten years, I'll find you and kill you.' In the end, I was more afraid

The Veil of Silence

of him than of my father, although he lived more than six hundred miles away, whereas my father was in Paris.

At every footstep in the street, I thought I caught sight of him. You can't imagine, the number of people I mistook for him! Moreover, my mother was curiously intent on keeping this obsession alive. Every summer following our trip, when she went to Algeria for a holiday, she returned with a stock of warnings. Back there, I had become a taboo subject: Mohand would not tolerate anyone speaking about me in his presence. He, on the contrary, never missed an opportunity of renewing his promise to come and stab me to death one day. The worst thing for me was having to give up any idea of attending Setsi Fatima's funeral. I had had to avoid Ifigha when we were doing our documentary, but on this occasion I felt ready to brave the danger to see my grandmother for the last time. But everyone in the family dissuaded ne: my brother would never let me set foot with impunity in my native village. So the woman who had given me more happiness than anyone, departed without my being able to pay her my last respects. But her soul is always close to me . . .

Fortunately, in Paris, my many activities prevented my underlying panic from becoming a neurosis. I was living with my fear . . . but I was living in the fast lane. Olivier and I completed our short. It was called *Algeria Colours* and was short-listed at the Mannheim Film Festival in Germany. We immediately started work on *Ciné-City*, a fairly sophisticated documentary on towns, as 'revised and corrected' thanks to the art of the cinema. Three years later we began a full-length film on the condition of immigrant workers in France. The title was to be *Ali in Wonderland*. It required long interviews, researching numerous locations and thousands of discussions with North Africans living in France, to obtain as much realism as possible without thereby betraying or deforming the truth.

The Veil of Silence

Naturally, *Algeria Colours* and *Ciné-City* did not earn us enough for me to give up my office job. The salary was not huge and the days seemed endless, but the evenings brought a reward: several times a week I went off to the University of Vincennes to finish my degree in cinematography.

The atmosphere at the university and my début as a film-maker helped me over the hardest of my tasks: the responsibility for my mother, brothers and sisters. The children were becoming very difficult. I spent my free time – mornings, evenings when I was not at the university, weekends – lecturing them and trying to stop them running away and getting into all kinds of mischief. I encouraged them to take up sports, I enrolled some of them at the local theatre arts school, to keep them out of bad company which was only too common in the poor neighbourhoods to which we successively moved. Djamel, in particular, caused me a great deal of worry, as he showed a marked propensity for associating with drop-outs and delinquents.

In 1974, we had moved into a slightly more comfortable flat in a council block in Epinay-sur-Seine. My mother was not satisfied: she dreamed of a detached house with its own garden. I promised I'd find her a house one day, as soon as I could afford it. She sulked . . .

She became more and more sullen, almost totally depressed. For months I accompanied her to various doctors, running from one specialist to another for repeated examinations which all proved negative, as every one of her succession of illnesses was purely psychosomatic.

Nevertheless she ought to have felt better after 1974: her divorce decree had been made absolute, my father had gone back to Algeria, remarried and fathered more children and didn't worry about us any more. From now on my mother didn't have anything to fear from him, and I was freed from a part of my own fear: that which concerned him.

The Veil of Silence

That being said, as my father still omitted to pay mother a penny alimony, the entire financial burden continued to fall on me. Family allowances for the youngest children were inadequate. I spent my all meagre savings and expended all my strength. I was at the end of my tether. I took vitamins to keep me going and tranquilizers to help me sleep. I was anxious, under pressure and . . . rarely with Olivier, except for our film work. This frantic desire to take everything on myself, added to the absolute priority that I gave to my family, since they were dependent on me, got the better of our love for each other. At the end of '74 we decided to separate, although we still continued to work together on our film, *Ali in Wonderland*.

Then I went to live at my mother's, in the flat for which I undertook the expenses, but which it would never have occurred to me to call my home. This solution seemed the most economical, and the most convenient for my role as 'mentor-guardian-probation officer'.

I shared a room with my sister Fatima, who had also come home to our mother's, after living by herself for a short time. I was very fond of her, I felt she was not strong, and I was distressed to see her show so little taste for study. I tried to drag her off to the university, in vain; you can't go against people's natures.

On the other hand, when I introduced her to a young Algerian journalist acquaintance of mine, she was all eagerness. They got married and the whole family congratulated Fatima. Mother never tired of praising her son-in-law. That he proved to be a 'decent' young man, counted for much less in these praises than the fact that he was Algerian, and a Kabyle to boot. My mother had finally married one of her daughters according to tradition, with an Arab – what am I saying? – with a Berber; so she had done her duty. When people, especially those in Ifigha, asked her, 'What's become of Djura, the eldest? Why isn't she married?'

The Veil of Silence

She simply replied, 'Djura? She's taking care of her sisters and brothers.'

In this way she hoped that they would condone my prolonged – or disguised – celibacy.

Amar married a French girl . . . without any objections being raised. To think that our people only obeyed the letter of the law where females were concerned. I was even asked to book a smart banqueting room for the reception, in a restaurant in Enghien, opposite the casino. We had to do the correct thing to be a credit to my brother and his in-laws. Actually, I found this atmosphere of understanding very gratifying: I had no desire for my brothers and sisters to experience my own past difficulties.

Belaîd, for his part, soon went off to the South-West of France with a woman much older than himself – a Frenchwoman also – who had one child, and gave him several more.

My mother ought to have been delighted to see her offspring leaving the nest: she only became all the more depressed. However there still remained four adolescents in Epinay, who were my responsibility as before. The newly-weds were too busy saving to set up their own home and we never saw the colour of their money. There's no doubt about it, I was the only one to respect the old traditions of mutual family assistance, I who – according to my father and brother – 'had infringed the laws' of our community. I did not feel any bitterness; I did what I deemed natural, and I did it lovingly. I was also happy that I had now obtained my degree and could practise my chosen profession. My ex-companion and I, who had remained good friends, had just finished our film.

1976: 'Ali' – or 'Djura in Wonderland'? I was indeed in

The Veil of Silence

seventh heaven. Algeria invited me to present the film at the Pan-African Festival, at which film-makers from the whole of Africa would be present. I was to lead the discussion after the showing at the Algerian Film Institute. I was proud to be able to do, in my turn, what Godard, Robbe-Grillet and Fassbinder had done before me, in this same place. The AFI, with its reputation for its uncompromising audiences! Algeria, calling on me, when I thought myself unknown!

Naturally, my joy was not unclouded. First, it was the end of the friendship between Olivier and myself. Olivier, co-director of the film, was deeply hurt and bitter at not being invited to this event. However much I tried to explain to him that this festival was for African film-makers, so it was normal for them to invite me as I was an African, he took this very badly and our relationship suffered.

And then, fear surfaced again. Algeria, Mohand, the death threat if I set foot on my native soil . . . Would I have to put up with this all my life? I took the risk and went to Algiers. I was very pleased with myself for being so brave and, at the same time, somewhat ashamed: I had not been so brave when Setsi Fatima died. I asked her forgiveness in my prayers. It is true that this time, I was going to the capital and not to Ifigha, my sacrosanct native village, where the affront of my presence would have been even more intolerable to my eldest brother.

All the same, during the whole showing of *Ali in Wonderland*, I scanned the auditorium in the darkness. Usually, all people responsible for the films do this to try to guess at the audience reaction. But I was trying to pick out Mohand . . .

An Algerian film-critic friend, in whom I confided, sat next to me to reassure me. But who could reassure me? Who could protect me effectively from my brother? After all, my fellow film-makers were not aware of the threat hanging over me, and the audience even less so.

The Veil of Silence

Suddenly I glimpsed at the back of the auditorium a silhouette which reminded me of Mohand. I began to tremble . . . All sorts of mad ideas ran through my mind. To escape just before the end, for example . . . But what would the organizers think of this director who took French leave before the discussion which she was supposed to lead?

And what if I myself sparked off the scandal? I would rush onto the stage, announce that I had made this film, and that there was someone here who wanted to destroy me. Who wanted to kill me, because of my activities, the ideas which I stood for. I would challenge the intellectuals present, explaining to them that sooner or later they would have to study the condition of women in their own country. Never mind about *Ali in Wonderland*: the problem of women seemed much more vital for the moment than the difficulties of immigration. Then I would point out my brother and we'd see what he'd find to reply . . . or to do.

Then, losing my head altogether, I returned to my first idea: to make a run for it . . . I sneaked into the central aisle and crept, bent double, towards the exit. Then I passed an Algerian *cinéaste* I knew well and who was astonished at my behaviour. I told him of my terror . . . He drew himself up to the limit of his massive corpulence, which would have impressed most people, and said quite loudly, rolling his Rs, 'You've nothing to be afrrraid of!'

Then he gently took me by the arm and quickly ushered me towards the screen; the film had just ended, the lights went up and my 'bodyguard' introduced me to the audience.

Applause broke out on all sides. I had regained my courage and gazed out into the auditorium with a determined expression, holding my head high. I looked especially at the spot where I thought I'd caught sight of Mohand. Had

The Veil of Silence

he left? Had I been mistaken? I heaved a sigh of relief when the discussion began . . .

Immediately, an old gentleman in a turban stood up. I recognized Momo, one of the pillars of the Film Institute, whose criticisms were particularly feared. A strange person, Momo, respected in spite of his eccentricity. He was a poet and he did readings of his works which he brought on to the stage in a shopping basket mixed up with oranges! That did not prevent the film-makers present from trembling, as he was always the first to give his verdict, which was not always favourable. The fate of the work being judged depended on his few words, for most often the audience went by his opinion. You can imagine my state when he began to speak.

'Sister Djura's film,' he said, 'is a powerful study of emigration. The image at the end is very successful, very symbolic, where you see the people who eat the oysters, those who open them and serve them on a dish, and those who collect them in dustbins. I like this film very much.'

He turned on his heels and was not seen again. I could have kissed him! He had just put out the red carpet for me, marking my success.

The rest of the discussion was very animated, degenerating even for a brief moment into acrimony between opposing cliques who were used to sowing discord.

Numerous friends accompanied me to my hotel. In the foyer, I had another good look round to inspect the spot. I was even tempted to confide in my friends who surrounded me to say goodbye. But I didn't like talking about my own problems . . . Only my one film-critic friend was in the know about my dramatic mishaps and adventures. He kept saying, 'Why do you work like mad looking for scenarios? The story of your life is the best film-script I know. That's the film you ought to make.'

The Veil of Silence

But at the time I had no desire to film or write my autobiography. No doubt it needed the worst to happen to me before I could try finally to exorcize the past.

Strangely enough, *Ali in Wonderland*, my first full-length film, was to decide my career – as a singer! And my life as a woman . . .

Although Olivier and I had split up as lovers some time ago, we were still working together on finishing the editing. The problem then arose of finding appropriate music to illustrate our pictorial portrayal. This was, obviously, before my trip to Algiers, since the work on the film was not yet completed.

I suddenly thought of Djamel Allam, the Kabyle singer. He was willing to let me use the tapes of his songs and gave me the address of his manager, Hervé Lacroix, who would obtain them for me.

So I rang this gentleman, who told me I could come that same evening about seven o'clock if I liked, and fetch the tapes from his home. He lived on the Ile Saint-Louis.

That day, unfortunately, I missed my train in Epinay and arrived at the Ile Saint Louis nearly an hour late . . . Strange as it may seem, I did not know this magical spot. One cannot dash from Vincennes to the most outlying suburbs, in search of locations in dormitory-housing-estates or Arab shantytowns, and at the same time explore Paris and its most beautiful places.

The Veil of Silence

I suddenly felt I was in another world. Night had just fallen and the lighted lamps gave the streets a provincial look, very 'village fête'. Moreover there was some sort of festive event going on: a very important private viewing which was attracting crowds, casually chic, discerning, off-beat. The lights were still on in all the galleries, and I felt inclined to roam around too . . . However, it was out of the question: I already felt sufficiently embarrassed at turning up at a stranger's house at dinner-time.

I eventually arrived at 55 rue Saint-Louis-en-l'Ile, where Hervé Lacroix had a ground-floor flat. I rang: no reply. The shutters were closed, however I could see light inside. I ought to have left, but I'd come too far not to persist; I hammered on the door.

It was finally opened by a tall, handsome young man, tanned as if he'd recently returned from a holiday. I was a bit surprised: I'd imagined I'd find a typical 'backer', a man in his fifties, imposing, paternal even. And here was a fellow of my own age, dressed in white jeans, smiling, casual. He asked me in . . .

I'd scarcely set foot inside his flat than the island was plunged into darkness by a power failure, a rather unusual occurrence only a few yards from the home of ex-president Pompidou, whose neighbours enjoyed the benefit of an emergency electricity supply.

'So, you're in the habit of blowing fuses, are you?' exclaimed my host with a laugh. 'Wait, I'll go and get a candlestick . . .'

I wasn't used to Parisian humour. Nor was I used to masculine familiarity, in spite of having lived with Olivier. The two of us were alone in the dark, and I felt some misgivings.

So, as soon as the lights came on again, I was ready to leave and announced, with scant courtesy, 'Okay, if you give me the tapes I'll be off.'

The Veil of Silence

Hervé made no comment, simply suggesting, 'Would you like to go out for a drink somewhere?'

'Out . . . somewhere'? I accepted . . . We went to the corner café. He explained that when I didn't turn up, he'd preferred to shut himself in. He knew nearly all the inhabitants of the island, but didn't care for social events. And seeing the atmosphere that evening, he was sure a crowd of cronies would come bothering him, begging him to join them.

We talked, and as we got to know more about each other, we felt a a mutual attraction. Not a superficial attraction: an instinctive realization that we were on the same wave-length, something which has stood the test of time. We promised to meet again and became close friends, then lovers, but this was no casual affair.

Hervé stood for everything that attracted me. he was an artist, a genuine one. As a talent-spotter he was quite unlike the average impresario, all bluff and percentages. When he believed in someone, there were no half measures. Money scarcely mattered to him, any more than to me. Everything that he earned, he immediately re-invested in his work. He had started working at the age of twenty in the Ranelagh Theatre, where he had come across Rufus and Higelin in the early stages of their careers, been an admirer of Diana Ross and associated with American groups, like the Temptations. That was when he was infected with the virus of show-business . . .

He had an inexhaustible general knowledge which fascinated me. He was interested in a host of things and he had a passion for Algeria. I have to admit at this juncture, that both of the men with whom I have lived were genuinely attracted to my country: Olivier, in his capacity as architect and film-maker, Hervé probably on a vaster and deeper historical and cultural level.

Our first journey together as lovers allowed me to

The Veil of Silence

discover strange coincidences between us, due perhaps to chance, if chance exists.

Hervé was a Breton. Saracen invasions cannot be said to have left their mark on this province, and yet the day he took me to his native region I had a colossal surprise . . .

We had first had a very pleasant drive towards his birthplace, the village of Saint-Quay-Portrieux, a spa on the Côtes-du-Nord . . . As I had no idea how beautiful this part of France is, I only expected one thing of Brittany: to see artichokes, my favourite vegetable.

Miles and miles and nothing . . . Then, suddenly: 'I can see one, I can see one!' I cried in delight.

'What are you talking about?' asked Hervé.

'Artichokes, of course! We're in artichoke country, aren't we?'

'There are plenty more interesting phenomena,' he replied with a smile.

Indeed, there was the sea. The Breton sea, wild and angry, difficult, changing, spectacular . . . Then, there was his grandmother's house. She had partly brought him up, just as mine had pampered me, already the first thing our childhoods had in common. And then, opposite this house, there rose up before me, like an apparition, an oriental castle with a minaret, arabesques round the doors and richly decorated windows.

'An eccentric at the turn of the century had it built for a countess he was madly in love with,' Hervé informed me. 'And look at the island just opposite; it's called the "Ile de la Comtesse". And that castle is the Château de Calan.'

The Château de Calan had me transfixed with excitement. To find something here from my homeland! I couldn't help seeing this as a good omen . . .

We found out that the castle was for sale. Alas! we couldn't afford to buy it, even 'for a song' as the estate

The Veil of Silence

agents said. I prayed it might somehow revert to me one day, or that Hervé might acquire it, or we might . . .

In fact, a few years later, it was sold to a speculator who transformed it into a hotel-restaurant. Blocks of one-room flats with huge bay windows were built, disfiguring the immediate surroundings, but the castle remained intact and the new owner was kind enough to let me visit the main hall. The tiling alone would have turned any king of Arabia pale with envy. And the gilded mosaics round the fireplace are in keeping with the magnificence of the whole.

For the moment, it was incredible: while showing me his roots, Hervé let me discover my own again.

It might be thought that there is much facile romanticism in these reflections, as always when one is in love. Nevertheless, later, when I was doing a recording with Alan Stivell, and singing on another occasion with Gilles Servat – both pure pedigree Bretons – I had plenty of time to realize, quite objectively, that Breton and Berber music have much in common. In the sharpness of the sounds, the resonance of the instruments, the relentlessly haunting melodies.

At any rate, at the time of our first escapade, when I was very much in love, I told myself that there was nothing surprising in the encounter between this fair-haired, blue-eyed Breton and the black-eyed Berber woman, if only for them to go for a picnic at the foot of a minaret, planted on Celtic soil, on the Ile de la Comtesse.

In addition to these many reasons for my being attracted to Hervé, another aspect of his character delighted me: his generosity. He lent people everything: his guitar, his flat, his clothes. Consequently, he perfectly understood my devotion to my family. He thought it splendid the way I took on so many responsibilities at once; I even think this made him proud of me. Olivier had put up with the state of affairs very nicely and with the utmost understanding, now Hervé soon showed himself ready to take the whole situation on board. He came to see my mother, my brothers and sisters, delighted to find himself accepted as a member of the family. He was very fond of them all, and expected us both to help them.

This generosity of heart and mind was to contribute to our downfall, but in 1976 we were still unaware of this.

Shortly after we met, Hervé had the idea of getting me to sing. He'd read the poems I'd written at Hussen Dey, I was by nature gay, spontaneous, I adored singing to myself; he had the feeling that something would come of it if I performed in public.

At first I didn't take his suggestions seriously and I must admit I wasn't very tempted. The traces of paterno-fraternal indoctrination? I didn't feel the idea of becoming a singer would do anything for my self-esteem. An opera singer, perhaps, but that was not my register.

Hervé pointed out that Brassens, Montand, Billie Holiday, were also great artistes in their way. And what about Taos Amrouche and Um Kalthoum?

Only, what about the cinema? After all, I'd made quite a good beginning; must I give it all up? I was thinking of making a film about the condition of women in my homeland. An enormous undertaking – and mountains of difficulties. Where would I find the necessary funding? And by whom would this provocative documentary be seen? Certainly not by Algerian women, the ones who would be directly concerned, but who would be shut up at

The Veil of Silence

home in this instance. Moreover the film itself would have every chance of being banned in Algeria. As for France, the work would perhaps be distributed on 'fringe' circuits, classed as an 'experimental art film', thereby preaching to the converted, and not to the public at large.

I've still not abandoned this idea but Hervé pointed out to me at the time that, in view of the predictable obstacles to making a film of this sort, singing would be a good way of expressing what I had to say, and letting it be heard quicker and more easily.

That was the trigger factor: I agreed to sing . . . The first time I had gone to Hervé's looking for music for *Ali in Wonderland*, I had been in search of voices: now I had just found my own.

A voice, and a way forward . . . For me, the way for my inspiration was marked out from birth. The links in the chain of the dog's life I had led had just joined together with a strangely encouraging logic. I was a young Algerian, in love with Berber traditions, but equally concerned about woman's place in modern society. I had suffered, like my female compatriots, from the social, political and family constraints which still persisted, in spite of claims to progress. It had always been my wish to stir things up, even when I did nothing more than timidly teach the girls at Tala-Gala an embryo feminine solidarity.

Well, I'd broaden the debate! I'd attempt to drag all Algerian girls into my struggle, and those from all North Africa, the whole of Africa, girls and women from other Arab countries, and even some from the West whose light was still hidden under a bushel. I would be like Kahina: with my songs I would raise a veritable army, loyal to the cultural wealth of our countries and yet rebelling against the omnipotence of an outdated patriarchy.

The Veil of Silence

So much for the theory, only we were no longer at the time of King Tabat, and I was alone. And I did not want to be seen as a solitary committed singer. I wanted us to be a group. A small group to begin with, but a group; I had to spread a common message and not do a star turn.

'We'll call ourselves 'Djurdjura',' I declared to Hervé one day.

'That sounds good,' he observed.

For me it had the echo of a thousand childhood memories, and the sounds of the first battles for Algerian independence. Battles in which women had taken a massive, courageous part. Djamila Boupacha, Djamila Bouhired, our mothers and grandmothers who shook their fists in the streets and country roads, shouting, 'Long live Algeria!' and uttering yuyus. What had become of these 'revolutionaries' now? The heroines had been forgotten and the others had been sent home without anything having changed for them. Basically, the women who participated in the French Revolution in the past had suffered the same fate, with this difference that their 'condition' – albeit dependent – compared to ours, was much more comfortable.

Only, in the West, there had been 1968 and the feminist movement; with the excesses that every social upheaval no doubt involves, but bringing an improvement in the condition of women that no-one could deny. I had the luck to be brought up in a Western country; I was at the crossroads of two cultures, I could draw the inspiration for my compositions from these two sources. Not denying the past nor my origins, but making them shine with the light of a brighter future.

For that, it would not be enough to perform as a 'folksy' group: we would have to compose new songs, inspired by the old ones, with added suggestions for future developments. That need be no problem, I would go back

The Veil of Silence

to the fountainhead and, as for the future, I'd rely on my own inspiration.

I set to work with enthusiasm, while still continuing with my 'bread-and-butter' work to maintain my family.
 How glad I was of my stay in Ifigha and Tala-Gala, in 1968, which had helped me to master my mother tongue! For there was no question of our singing in any language but Kabyle, at least in the majority of my songs . . .
 How grateful I was to my old cousins in Tala-Gala for singing to me and stocking my memory with all the dancing refrains and other treasures of the region! I added to this holiday documentation by research at the Bibliothèque Nationale. I found many Berber poems collected by Hanoteau and Letourneux during the colonial period: songs of joy, war-songs, melancholy or ironical airs, but for the most part veritables cries of revolt uttered by women against their condition. *'Merci, ma mère, vous m'avez obligée à épouser un hibou'* . . . ('Thank you, mother, you forced me to marry an owl'). Feminist compositions, some of which 'cries' I had heard in the region, only these were murmured during domestic tasks, when the women were among themselves, far from men . . .
 Well then, our slogan for Djurdjura would be, 'We sing aloud what our mothers hummed under their breath.' And every man would recognize his mother, his wife, his own daughter and their fate, in my more or less protest poems.
 Nevertheless, I did not want simply to sow revolt, I wanted my compositions to bring smiles and hope, and for them to express the traditional charm of our lovely country. I mingled, to the best of my ability, the riches of my country's heritage with the resources of world music.

The Veil of Silence

I had an innate sense of melody and an instinct for our rhythms. My mother couldn't get over the fact that she recognized familiar memories of her youth in the songs and dances that I composed.

To say she was delighted to see me 'tread the boards' would however be totally untrue . . . She constantly repeated the same old story, 'What will the people of Ifigha say when they hear about this! I'll never dare show my face in the village again . . .'

Then I reminded her of her own forced marriage, of the times she'd been punished for running away, the drudgery she'd endured, her repeated pregnancies, the blows she'd received. I made her admit that if she were my age, she too would like to make known the pitiful condition that was inflicted on so many of us. I told her that by singing in this way I wanted to bear witness to her own sufferings.

Then I finally won her over by adding that by the time our notoriety reached Kabylia much water would have flowed under the bridges. First we had to try. If we failed, nobody back home would know anything about it. And if success crossed the seas . . . well, you don't become the laughing-stock of a village if your daughter is successful.

We still had to set up Djurdjura, and I still had no co-performers . . . Then I lured my sister Fatima into the venture. She took it up at first for fun, then had to set to work. She didn't speak Kabyle very well; I taught her the intonations, the lyrics, the pronunciation . . .

Then I got mother's permission to enrol my aunt, her young sister, not much older than me. My aunt had

The Veil of Silence

been married but her husband had repudiated her one week after the wedding. She hadn't stirred from her village for years, then one day she had left for France on the pretext of needing dental treatment. With us, a single woman always needed a pretext to be allowed to travel . . .

So Aunt J—, who had come to Paris for three months, had already been there for five years . . . and still had trouble with her gums! She was an extraordinary woman, extremely adaptable. She was crazy with joy at the idea of singing. Naturally she spoke our native language fluently, and she improvised on the most varied rhythms as if she was still just enjoying herself at a village wedding. In a word, she brought a touch of popular authenticity which taught me – the little 'Parisian' – a great deal. We all three wore the traditional gandoura, in addition to the red and gold *fouta*, this sort of apron-cum-handtowel, which was to become in some respects the symbol of our struggle.

Hervé, for his part, helped me to find musicians. I needed typical percussions – *derboukas* and *bendirs* – but also a keyboard, flute, drum-kit, bass guitar and electric guitar. Five or six instrumentalists at least, not easy to unearth.

Hervé also looked for a venue and got busy immediately with publicity for Djurdjura. With the result that, one evening, he announced out of the blue that he'd just signed a contract for a performance on 15 May 1977, at La Tombe,[1] near Montereau. Panic! there were barely two months left to put the finishing touches to the

---

[1] In a letter to the translator the author writes: 'To put on your first performance in a town called La Tombe is as if you were to be born in a tomb; you can't begin any lower and you can only rise higher.' (Trans.)

programme, to last three-quarters of an hour to begin with . . .

I didn't have as much stage fright as I'd thought, as it was an open-air festival, popular, friendly, a bit like our festivities in Ifigha, on a larger scale. Everything was ready, the musicians, the singers, their costumes and the words of women speaking out . . .

I forgot my mother's new equivocations: she had said, the previous evening, 'Just you be careful! Most of the people at this sort of gathering are immigrants. How will they take this? The men I mean . . . You risk being booed off the platform and having bottles thrown at you.'

You have to admit that in 1977, an immigrant paterfamilias was hardly used to hearing accusations about the lives of his daughters, sisters and wife. But were we not there to get things changed?

No-one threw bottles and it was a triumph, as much with the North Africans as with the French in the audience, for whom Djurdjura was an astonishing and satirical discovery. The encouragements I received that day made me forget the sleepless nights that had preceded the event. I felt myself blossom in this new form of expression. A psychiatrist friend said to me, 'Anyone would think you'd been doing this all your life. Only, it's not surprising: your grandmother put you on show from the first day of your birth, according to what you told me.'

I thought with emotion of Setsi Fatima.

Hervé did not let me rest on my laurels. He drew up programmes for new performances, and decided to improve

The Veil of Silence

the 'orchestral' side of the production. Serious, traditional North African musicians were a rare commodity. And besides, they were men: accompanying my 'subversive' lyrics didn't appeal to all of them. What is more, three quarters of them behaved like amateurs, arriving late for rehearsals and sometimes, the last straw, forgetting to turn up for performances! That could not go on.

Fortunately, that year, Hervé was also managing a certain number of performers in Algeria, in collaboration with the Ministry of Culture. He also had the opportunity of meeting the conductor of the Algerian Radio and Television Orchestra, Boudjemia Merzak, who soon after came to settle in France.

He and Hervé had become friends; we explained our musical problems to him. Merzak was very familiar with the North African musical circles in France and the problems associated with them . . . He advised us not necessarily to select North Africans. We'd do better to look also to musicians of other nationalities – provided that they were genuine professionals – and he would be responsible himself for teaching them our melodic styles.

Finally, the only Algerian remaining in the group was our faithful friend Rabah Khalfa, the best percussionist in the Maghreb. The others were, and still are, French – Bretons (they insist on this distinction!) – Americans, all interested in our venture, all becoming specialists in Berber music, all talented, conscientious, adorable . . .

Confident in this new team, Hervé – who certainly likes taking new risks – organized a show with Djurdjura and the Kabyle singer Idir, for 23 January 1978, at Olympia. No North African artist had ever performed on this prestigious stage, and the immigrant population had scarcely ever had the opportunity of setting foot in this theatre. North Africans were in the habit of going to applaud their

The Veil of Silence

singers in 'cultural' centres that were set aside for them: The Sonacotra[1] centres.

For me, it was nerve-wracking. I liked risks but I thought Olympia was perhaps premature all the same. Hervé reassured me: we were ready for everything.

Everything, except the unpredictable: my mother took this good news as a disaster and formally forbade her sister to perform in such a place which was too well known for her taste. She considered herself responsible for my aunt's reputation, and if she'd been of the opinion that our little performances had up till now passed unnoticed, she knew it would not be the same in the most famous Parisian music-hall.

'Uncles, aunts, cousins, all those who live in Paris will be there and they'll recognize her,' she explained to me. 'Her mother and brothers back home will get to hear of it, they'll never forgive her for such a disgrace, nor me!'

It was all starting again . . . My aunt was over thirty, but she was still a minor. I argued till I was blue in the face, even suggesting that she wear a mask to preserve her anonymity. It was no use; she had to leave us overnight . . . and we never saw her again.

At the shortest possible notice I had to replace that member of the group who I still call 'my shooting star'. I contacted several Algerian girls, whose parents refused my offers. Then I asked my mother to let my young sister Malha help us out. Malha was twenty, she was born in France, understood Kabyle but couldn't speak it. I had to

---

[1] Sonacotra: Acronym for Société Nationale de Construction de Logements pour Travailleurs (National Society for Construction of Housing for Workers), by implication immigrant workers, then by extension applied to the workers themselves, living in the sub-economic flats built to house them. (Trans.)

The Veil of Silence

teach her everything, the poems, the music – and how to dress. Malha didn't care a damn about her appearance, slopping about all day in jeans and trainers. It was quite a business to get her to put on make-up, wear long dresses, jewellery and a *fouta*! To make things worse, she was still at the lycée and hadn't much time for rehearsals.

No matter, on 23 January, as soon as she got out of school, she made her way stout-heartedly to Olympia . . .

Hervé came to my dressing-room to tell me there were enormous crowds outside, queuing up for tickets. I shrugged. 'It can't be for us. They're booking for Aznavour, next week.'

'The day when there's a full house for you here, you won't need me any more,' Hervé murmured.

I knew perfectly well I'd always need him as my life's companion, and as co-pilot for my professional life.

Besides, he'd been right: gradually the people waiting outside poured into the auditorium, till it was crowded with French people as well as immigrants. Behind the curtain I paced up and down, a prey to stage fright. A thing which up till then had seemed easy, was now a problem. We had mostly performed in the open air, in the festival atmosphere I loved and knew from my childhood. Mistakes passed unnoticed in the surrounding euphoria, sometimes amid the hubbub of applause. Whereas here, you could hear a fly buzzing and pick up the slightest wrong note. We were going to be right in the limelight, they'd pick us to pieces, pass sentence on us. And suppose the whole thing was a flop? Suppose they pelted us with tomatoes? Suppose . . .

'You're on!'

The spot-lights picked us up opposite the prompter's side and followed us to the middle of the stage. Suddenly thunderous applause broke out . . . I wasn't quite sure what was happening, but I felt myself galvanized into

The Veil of Silence

action, standing tall, proud, as if filled with sunshine. The musicians were there, reassuring. My sisters stood one on each side of me. I had told them, 'Don't be afraid, and whatever happens, follow me' . . . I glanced at them from time to time during the performance, to indicate that we were in this together. There was total symbiosis, and Olympia was a tremendous success.

Djurdjura was 'launched', as my friends said, although I didn't let myself be taken in by the term. It simply meant that we had exchanged amateur status for that of professionals, and become thereby exposed to severe critical judgement. There was no longer any question of improvising, giving slipshod performances, briefly, any lowering of standards.

I was determined to make every sacrifice to this end, confident that I would always draw inspiration from the dazzling memories of my native Kabylia and the desire to offer a little more freedom to women like myself. And besides, I was not fighting alone. Did I not have the support of my sisters, to whom I'd taught our art, and the possible backing of Algeria, whose culture I was making known through my compositions?

However, it was these two 'sources of consolation' which were to let me down in the first place, and which attempted subsequently to clip my wings.

The very next day after our Olympia appearance, I called Fatima and Mahla together and explained to them that

The Veil of Silence

we'd have to make ourselves available in future for the various gala performances which wouldn't fail to ensue, and above all, we must rehearse more often, whatever additional activities we might have. They looked at me unenthusiastically. Gala performances, the stage, sure – that was fun. But work was another matter . . .

Problems began immediately. They came to rehearsals when they felt like it. Hervé, meanwhile, had set up a small recording company for us. The registered office of this company was an old converted barn, fitted out from bits and pieces, where Hervé and I also lived. After this acquisition, we qualified in their eyes as employers, not to say profiteers, whereas we paid all the expenses and negotiated decent fees for my sisters and the musicians. The latter never grumbled; my sisters on the other hand did, behaving like spoilt children. They stormed off the stage for no justifiable reason, returned in tears and indulged in emotional blackmail to which I too often yielded. This atmosphere reduced Hervé to despair. He was signing contracts all over France, never sure if the 'youngsters' would turn up. He hardly dared set up more ambitious plans; tours abroad, for example. We were endlessly at the mercy of adolescent crises which put the futures of Djurdjura and the instrumentalists at risk.

I did my best to persuade my sisters of the attractions of our career, the merits of our mission; they couldn't give a damn. In fact, they wanted all the advantages, without accepting the hardships. They adored the recognition, the flattery, the applause, the flowers; but found the tiring journeys, early morning interviews, too-short nights in second-rate hotels a bore and a nuisance to put up with. They wouldn't accept any comments Hervé or I were naturally obliged to make. They wished 'to settle comfortably in an uncomfortable profession', to quote Louis Jouvet's celebrated phrase. They imagined, like many

The Veil of Silence

beginners who do not really have the driving force, that a first success or a well-received first recording represents the promise of a perpetual fairyland.

So Djurdjura took off with Hervé, as well as me, never sure what would happen from one day to the next. A few days before our appearance at the Théâtre de la Ville, in March 1979, which coincided with the publication of our first album, Malha decided to leave us without notice. I immediately had to train a substitute, who was fortunately fairly talented, with whom I rehearsed through the night. Hervé, for his part, had troubles with the producer of the show on account of this defection. What is more, he had to pay out of his own pocket to have posters, press hand-outs, photographs and all the publicity material reprinted at the last minute.

Fatima was a bit more reasonable, but not very motivated for all that. She preferred singing to working in an office, and probably hoped to earn a small fortune in this career. Only she didn't put her heart and soul into it. Maybe she stayed out of affection for me, at least that's what I thought . . . I was very fond of her. She was the closest to me of all my sisters, always in cahoots with me. Our adolescence had corresponded with the hardest period of our family life. We'd suffered together, even if I'd been the one to take the brunt of the mindless cruelty of my own kith and kin. I wanted us to share some happiness from now on. Besides, we'd had some good times together, since we lived quite near each other. I confessed to her my worries about my brothers and the other sisters, especially my youngest brothers, who were big now but didn't seem too worried about looking for work. Fatima was the only one to tell me I was doing too much, and that I'd do better to consider myself a bit. I think she was frankly exasperated when, in 1980, Malha returned repentant to the fold and I agreed to take her back.

The Veil of Silence

Fatima was right. After promising, swearing she wouldn't run out on us again, saying she'd thought things over, she was more mature, she'd opted for our 'cause', a few months later Mahla left a second time without warning.

And there I was, trying to make up a team once more. From 1977 to 1985 I spent more time training substitutes than perfecting the basic work. The way things were going, Djurdjura ought gradually to have faded away. But the need to make a statement, the wish to communicate through poetry and music, were stronger than anything with me. The stage and the audience changed my life for the better. My sensibility found the way of expressing itself, I was no longer so withdrawn, I became more outgoing and had the feeling I was doing something useful. That, in my eyes, was worth the effort needed to overcome all obstacles.

After Malha, Hervé and I took Djamila, the baby of the family, in hand. She didn't have to be asked twice to join us; she was only too happy to leave school, which she detested. She also hoped to get away from the atmosphere of the home, where she was permanently in conflict with my mother and brothers. She was sixteen and I thought her enchanting. What is more, she was very talented. When she was quite young, I'd enrolled her for music and dancing courses at the Epinay municipal academy for the arts. She was passionately keen on dancing and for some time I thought she'd make a career of it. But she gave it up through lack of perseverance. I attributed this to her difficult childhood, her loneliness in such a large family, in spite of the attentions I lavished on her.

Now we were there to support her and we had faith in her. The musicians made a fuss of her and treated her like their little mascot, I taught her the songs, the language, just

The Veil of Silence

as I'd done with the others. I spent days talking to her in Kabyle, I again paid for singing and piano lessons for her. I dragged her off with Fatima to drama courses, to lessons in modern, classical, African and even Indian dancing, to enrich our artistic culture and my own personal inspiration and at the same time.

Djamila's enthusiasm lasted a few months, then she jibbed at all this 'schoolwork', as she called it, and began to oppose me, just like my young brothers, with my mother sometimes joining in the chorus. Except possibly Fatima, they all considered everything I did for them as their rightful due and quite normal. I wore myself out keeping the promise I'd made years before: to be responsible for my little family until they were all grown-up, and to take care of my mother, who was still as depressed as ever and no warmer towards me than in the past.

Fortunately, there was Hervé, and the miracle of the performances. Although I nearly died of stage fright in the wings, I felt myself come to life once the spotlights were on me. From Lille to Carthage, in France as well as abroad, the public never failed us. From 1980 to 1982, Djurdjura made great and promising strides. Tour followed tour. The media gave us wide coverage. More and more women and girls turned up, North Africans as well as others. For those who didn't understand our language, translations of my words were given in between each song, and the message went down well.

My heart beat in time to the applause. I gathered up the audience's smiles, delight, astonishment, like so many bouquets. Many men looked at us with scarcely disguised admiration. One day, an immigrant in his fifties came on to the stage with a note. On it he'd written in clumsy letters, 'Long live the free Algerian woman!' I immediately read his message over the mike; the audience went mad.

I held my head high in the presence of these crowds, hieratic and proud, as if North African culture and North African women were uplifted through me. But in my heart, I was on my knees before these people who supported me and welcomed me with open arms. I had not felt loved in my childhood, and at a stroke I had everyone's love. To return this love, I gave myself unstintingly. I clapped my hands to the sound of the *derbouka*, my bracelets beat against my skin till I was covered with bruises. Every performance was a red-letter day . . . The audience, a mixture of all races and all ages, felt this and joined in the rejoicing by clapping their hands as well. Often children came and sat on the edge of the stage, beating time and coming to embrace us at the end of the performance. 'There is always a special communication between Djurdjura and their audience,' the reporters wrote.

What was communicated in the first place was emotion – the only essential thing for any artist to convey, the only truth, the only thing that's effective – which perhaps allowed my struggle to carry beyond the limits of the concert halls.

My struggle . . . I was fighting for the self-determination of Algerian women among others of our sisters in the same situation, so that they could to be freed from the interminable guardianship of their fathers, brothers, husbands. To those who repeated, as if they were giving lessons in morality, that women must remain the respectful guardians of traditions, I replied, 'Wrong! They are the keepers of popular culture; that's not the same thing.'

The Veil of Silence

Culture is the jewel in the people's crown, their common heritage. It can grow richer, if history permits, but it must remain, from its earliest beginnings, in everyone's memory. 'He who does not know whence he comes cannot know whither he goes,' wrote Gramsci . . . On the other hand, traditions represent many customs, both good and bad, which often need a good dusting-off, if you want to be able to be ready for progress.

While singing about this need, I was perfectly aware of the political implications of my words, hoping that other people – professional politicians – would take over from me in my beloved Algeria. I thought that perhaps, by listening to us, they would be inspired to lift the taboos faster, not in order to preach some sort of permissiveness, but to create harmony, a mixed masculine and feminine force, which would help our society to develop better.

This noble ambition, however, didn't seem to be to the liking of the Algerian government. They had been very pleased with *Ali in Wonderland,* but weren't interested in 'Fatma', neither as an immigrant nor an Algerian woman living in her native land. Yet, since the 1976 Charter, women had acquired, on paper, the same rights as men, but this had remained a dead letter. Their lives remained just as we satirized them in our performances.

So, the official circles took every opportunity of blocking our propaganda and of pouring scorn on my songs which dared to emphasize the most flagrant contradiction in the system: a claim to social equality to which the female half of the population was excluded.

Needless to add no-one invited Djurdjura to Algeria, no gala performance was allowed and our records were banned.

This prohibition, however, did not reflect the wishes of the people: they all bought our cassettes under the counter. A few distributors, including ONDA (the Algerian counterpart of SACEM[1]) shut their eyes to this pirating and profited from it. Too bad about my royalties; at least we were getting heard.

The better to discourage sympathizers, rumours were spread that Djurdjura represented opposition to the régime. Yet we had never got mixed up in that, neither I nor my sisters.

That being said, I couldn't help taking stock in private of our twenty-five years of independence. I am well aware that new-born – or resurrected – states need time for reconstruction, but really . . . this was a funny sort of reconstruction. Scarcities of nearly everything, unemployment, housing shortages, increasing delinquency, the biggest rise in the divorce rate in the world, the highest birth rate but also the most spectacular female suicide rate and frustration of young people: Sixty percent of the population ill-prepared for the future and yet who adore this country . . . Added to this, repression of any show of conflicting opinions, the FLN, the single party led by a hard core, supported by the all-powerful army, which produces military heads of state and justifies the legitimacy of power: however much you want 'not to get involved in politics' – to use the hallowed expression – you can't stop yourself thinking.

Only, once again, you hadn't the right to express these thoughts! What drove me to despair – and still does – was the ban on any criticism. 'Those who are not satisfied with our magnificent Algerian sunshine can go elsewhere,' President Boumedienne had stated . . .

Many Algerians had then left the country, some of them with the intention of forming an embryo opposition. They

[1]ONDA: Organisation Nationale de Diffusion Artistique.
SACEM: Société des Auteurs Compositeurs et Musiciens.

The Veil of Silence

were immediately accused of being in the pay of countries intent on destabilization. Yet the only thing they did was to denounce the complete absence of consultation: a one-party state, with one radio station, one television, at the service of a power which was educating the masses according to its own convictions – or its own ambitions, as some said bitterly.

These exiles also highlighted many of the problems arising from having Islam as the state religion, difficult to reconcile with socialist dogma. I myself am a Muslim but . . . Should we not re-read the Quran, as the Gospels should also be re-read? When in the Gospels it is written that a wife should be subject to her husband, there is the added proviso that the husband must also be subject to his wife. That part of the sentence has been skipped for centuries!

Be that as it may, in Algeria the wife remains at the mercy of the Quranic law, as it was interpreted at the beginning of Islam. In the absence of any structured secular legislation, it is the thousand-year-old Muslim legal system which has the force of law in the courts, accepting as an established fact the supremacy of the man, the possibility of his forbidding his wife to work outside the home, his right to repudiate her, to marry off his daughters without their consent, to outdo everyone else in punishing them, and even the right still to polygamy!

In such a context, it was easy to file my songs in the drawer labeled 'sacrilegous ideas'. The fact that my compositions were the vehicle for Berber culture was no more highly thought of than my 'feminism': as far as anything connected with the government was concerned, 'Berberitude' was considered synonymous with opposition, and many other artists had been permanently banned for having defended

The Veil of Silence

proud Barbary's cultural heritage. Had not Slimane Azem, the father of contemporary Kabyle songs – a subtle combination of La Fontaine and Georges Brassens – lived in exile all his life? Nearer to our own time, Mouloud Mammeri, the celebrated poet-custodian of the secrets of our language, was harried in his turn. One day, when on his way to give a lecture on Berber poetry, against which the students at Tizi-Ouzou raised a hue and cry, he was stopped by a police road-block and forced to turn back. This was what triggered off the first riots of the 'Berber Spring' of 1980. The student heirs of Jugurtha and Kahina-the-Rebel, who only wanted to express their right to differ, were violently suppressed. Many Kabyle poets, writers and singers were banished.

That is why I willingly agreed to become the vice-president of an association whose aim was to unite in harmonious creativity, across national frontiers, Kabyle, Chaouîa and Tuareg artistes, as well as all Arab-speakers. This association was called ACIMA.[1] We worked quite successfully for two years, then many members lost interest in the unifying mission, which nevertheless respected individual personalities, and ACIMA finally disappeared.

But I, for my part, did not give up fighting for the rest of my ideas. I had no ambition to be a politician, nor a liking for power, but no cause serving equality or justice left me indifferent. The cause of women and young girls in so many lands, mutilated, ridiculed, raped: the cause of children who die for lack of food or care; of Apartheid, of human beings in search of dignity, tortured or imprisoned in every latitude. I took part in conferences organized by Amnesty International, the League for Human Rights, MRAP,[2] Committees for the support of Algerian political

[1] Association Culturelle des Immigrés Artistes.
[2] Movement Contre le Racisme et pour l'Amitié entre les Peuples.

The Veil of Silence

prisoners and so many other organizations who asked me to take part in benefit galas which I never refused.

That infuriated my sisters. For, naturally, in such cases, we forfeited our fees and they considered my generosity eccentric. Then I had to go off once more in search of other singers. The audience became accustomed to seeing me carrying the banner of my convictions all alone, with a rota of female artistes around me. My sisters became bitterly jealous, accusing me of 'feathering my own nest', whereas I was simply leading a team in permanent dislocation, of which I was the sole motor force. Their desire for stardom, moreover, drove my dear little sisters to run down the contents of the show itself as well.

'It's not by endlessly warbling ditties about women and immigrants that we'll become stars!' Djamila let fly at me spitefully.

And yet, these 'ditties', which seemed to me rather nice poems, had changed her life very much for the better. She had discovered another world from that of our council flats, met interesting people, wore fine clothes, drank champagne, gave autographs. She forgot I was the one who'd given her the opportunity to behave so freely, by standing up to the despotism of the men of the family, at the risk of my life. She forgot that Hervé and I had taught her everything she knew about performing. She despised her origins; she already saw herself on the top rung of show-business.

Fatima was not so ambitious, but my mania for taking all the world's troubles to heart, on top of the family's troubles, got on her nerves and did not move her.

There resulted from all this dissension a tense and fairly unpleasant atmosphere. But in the presence of journalists,

The Veil of Silence

audiences and friends, I acted as if nothing were wrong, even if these quarrels undermined me from within. I didn't mention these difficulties to anyone. The main thing was for Djurdjura to survive and continue to spread its message everywhere.

'The House of Happiness' . . . I had just purchased it, in 1981, with my first royalties, plus the first profits from our recording company and a substantial bank loan. I was keeping my promise: at last my mother would be able to live in a large house, far from high-rise council flats.

Hervé and I, for our part, were beginning to fix up our barge on the Seine, delighted with this charming and unusual abode.

The house for my mother was in fact a magnificent seven-room villa, with cellar, garage, balconies, garden, surrounded by greenery and quiet, in Lardy, to the South of Paris.

'A pity there isn't an open fireplace,' said my mother.

I must confess that I was fairly stunned by this expression of gratitude, but all in all mother seemed very pleased and more optimistic than I'd seen her for a long time.

Djamel and Hakim, my young brothers would come and live with her here, removed from their 'gangs' in the council estates. Then they could seriously set about finding a job as well as achieving a certain stability.

Exactly the opposite occurred . . . My shiftless brothers settled down to their life of idleness more comfortably than ever, but continued to hang around with their former

The Veil of Silence

cronies. The youngest, Djamel, who had just turned eighteen, was becoming arrogant, violent, lording it over my mother and me, and threatening us. He rejected all proposals of work, and even refresher courses or youth training schemes that I offered to pay for. The situation became such hell that mother and I decided to send him to my married brother Amar, who might manage to instil some sense into him. Amar soon gave up this impossible task and packed Djamel off to Belaîd in the South-West of France, and he in turn eventually despatched him to Mohand, in Algiers.

Whereupon Mohand, who now had a fairly good situation, decided he too would build a house for my mother in Kabylia. I never knew if this was a belated gesture of filial love or a way of competing with me. What was certain was that from now on my mother swore only by this new house. She decided to leave straight away to supervise the work. At first she came back to France every three months, then every six months, then less and less frequently.

When she turned up in Lardy, she sang the praises of her Algerian existence, boasting of her eldest son's generosity. What he had just given her was much finer than all I'd done for her for twenty years, that is, giving her and her children the means of surviving. I suppressed the heartache that her off-hand ingratitude always caused me, pleased that she was happy between Paris and Ifigha, close to Mohand who she'd probably always loved more than any of us, and in good health.

From then on, the house in Lardy, for which I paid the bills and the various expenses, was to become a transit camp where they would all move in as the spirit moved

The Veil of Silence

them or according to the dictates of their changing fortunes. Djamila had been living there from the beginning, which saved her paying rent and allowed her to keep the whole of her earnings. Hakim had no intention of working and so was largely my responsibility. I continued to put money into an account to maintain some of the family. My mother, for her part, would ring me up from Algeria to ask for news, and take the opportunity to request me to hand over such and such a sum to certain of her friends who were passing through Paris, so as to repay money she'd borrowed over there. All that, plus the houseboat, and the expenses of the recording company, was beginning to impose a serious burden on our budget for Hervé and me. But no-one worried about that: once more, it was normal.

Everything was to seem normal to my family from now on, even the worst blackmail. On 1 April 1982, Djamel rang me to announce that he was back from Algiers. I replied that he could certainly stay in the house in Lardy.

'Obviously I'll go to the house!' he replied, as if it was a matter of course. 'But that's not the problem. I need money. You're a singer and you've got plenty. So you get me fifty thousand francs in cash and bring it to me in Lardy tomorrow. I'll be waiting for you.'

I thought this was an April Fool joke; it was only the beginning of the threats. He did indeed move into the house, which he considered belonged to him, and was waiting for me on a war-footing.

'Either you give us this money, or we'll do you in!' he declared.

Who was this 'us', this 'we'? Was he sent by Belaîd? Or by the oldest in Algiers, who nursed irreversable hatred towards me? Or by both of them? I don't know . . . I only know that Hervé delivered me from this racket with the help of a police inspector and Djamel made a getaway,

The Veil of Silence

going straight back to the South-West of France, as if by chance, and then on to Algiers. That is, rejoining Belaîd, then Mohand, both of whom, in my opinion, were in league with him.

My mother, who was in Algeria at that time of the year, and to whom I'd written, putting her in the picture, did not blaim Djamel in the slightest, according to what I heard. Did her everlasting fear of what people would say prompt her to hush the affair up? Was she so proud of having not just one, but two sons around her, that she didn't want anything to dim this supreme sense of well-being? Daughters don't count in the happiness of one's old age. They are made for other homes, to have sons in their turn, who will look after them later. As for me, I had neither any 'official' home, nor sons. I was a creature apart, the 'black sheep of the family', I suppose, but the one who nevertheless looked after everybody.

My sisters, for their part, enjoyed the greatest possible freedom, without having to suffer the 'punishment' I had endured for refusing to marry an unknown Arab and then going to live with a Frenchman. Fatima got divorced at the beginning of the 80s, leaving her Kabyle for a German, with whom she had a baby in 1984. She abandoned the group then and I went off once more in search of singers.

Djamila was still with Djurdjura at this time, and still living in Lardy. But she and Hakim had turned the house into a haunt of layabouts and scroungers, offering open house to all and sundry, giving noisy parties, transforming the villa into a permanent disco. The whole interior was falling to pieces and I wasn't surprised – in view of the type of creature haunting the place – to hear that the house had been burgled.

We discussed the matter with my mother, when she was able to ascertain the extent of the damage, and by common accord we agreed to sell the villa. I would find mother a

The Veil of Silence

smaller flat for when she visited France, which she did less and less frequently. So I put the house in the hands of two local estate agents. This was in 1985. While waiting to find a buyer, Djamila and Hakim would stay on there, after which I would try and make them face their responsibilities.

That was when Malha, whom we hadn't seen since she left the group in 1980, reappeared after five years silence. She beseeched me, she begged me again and again to forgive her . . . She explained that she too had left her first Kabyle husband and was now living with a Frenchman who had straightened her out. She explained that she felt more at ease with herself and had decided to make a fresh start – if I'd agree to take her back with Djurdjura.

My inherent maternal instincts let me be won over once again. And then I was experiencing so many rebuffs from the others that Malha's apparent affection consoled me a bit. I put her in the picture with what had been happening all these years: Fatima's departure, Djamel's attempted extortion racket, the havoc Hakim and Djamila were wreaking on the house, mother living in Algeria and having no scruples about leaving me responsible for all the finances as usual: she wept over my fate, assuring me that from now on I could count on her.

We had to argue for hours with Djamila before she would agree to let her sister back into the group.

'After all the trouble she's given you, you're prepared to welcome her with open arms?'

I explained that we were sisters, that we had to be forgiving. Djamila shrugged . . .

I had a soft spot for Djamila, 'my' baby. Had I not changed her nappies, rocked her to sleep, fed her like my own daughter? Nevertheless she was behaving worse

The Veil of Silence

and worse towards me. Did she want to make me suffer what she couldn't make my mother suffer any more, since she'd gone back to Kabylia? For some time she'd been calling me 'Mummy' . . . I thought at first that this was a transference of affection. But her insistence on throwing up 'Mummy' at me, at every opportunity, if possible in public, soon persuaded me of the contrary: she wanted to emphasize the difference in our ages and make me feel uncomfortable. I put her in the shade and this rivalry soon prompted attempts to seduce Hervé, which decency prevents me from describing.

Notwithstanding all this, she was right not to trust in Malha's promises. After a few months, the day before a very important television appearance, Malha announced that she was flying to Mauritius – for a holiday!

'I've been given the ticket, it's an opportunity not to be missed. And I must leave straight away, as I won't be able to travel later – I'm pregnant.'

'A funny way to announce such good news,' I replied coldly. 'But I don't see that's a valid reason for cancelling the TV broadcast. You can put off your trip for one day, can't you? And then you can do as you like; if you don't come back, I'll manage, as usual.'

She was annoyed, but appeared on the platform just the same, without addressing a word to anyone, then left on holiday and on her return rejoined the group, all smiles and, strangely enough, patched up her quarrel with Djamila – the better to try conclusions with me, as I was soon to discover.

One morning, in fact, Djamila phoned me on the houseboat, asking me to meet her at Malha's so that we could 'discuss things'. What did they want now? New costumes, higher fees?

When I got to Malha's, I'd scarcely put my foot inside the door than they both announced their joint decision to quit

The Veil of Silence

Djurdjura immediately, for good. Djamila had a charming way of explaining the reasons for their decision!

'We're fed up, you understand. And we want to dump you in the shit. Like that you won't be able to continue your rubbishy show. Your songs are rubbish, you're rubbish, Hervé's rubbish. And it's not with your trashy show that we'll become stars!'

Whereupon, she grabbed me by the collar and started to hit me. This baby who I'd held in my arms, raising her hand to me!

It was too much. I pushed her hand away firmly, and with a composure that I'd never have thought myself capable of, I said to both of them, 'You want to leave? Well go then. Good luck to you.'

And I departed, with my heart in shreds, my eyes soon filled with tears, but at the same time with a sense of relief. It had to finish like this. I'd had enough of begging them to work, to turn up punctually, to do their job correctly. There were other singers, who'd frequently helped me out, I'd manage with them.

Eventually I contacted one of my former substitute singers, I trained another new one, and everything went off perfectly. The atmosphere was different, more relaxed, and a hundred times more professional. The musicians themselves were delighted with the change. Our rehearsals were no longer an unpleasant chore but a real artistic exercise. How could I have poisoned my existence all those years by trying at all costs to work as a family in order to give my sisters a chance?

Besides, I'd made up my mind: I wasn't going to let my life be eroded any longer by my parasitical family. I was more than thirty-six, it was time I thought about myself, about Hervé, about the two of us. It was time for me to have a child myself, and start saving to be able to bring it up.

I let my brothers and sisters know that I would give no more money to any of them. They were young, in perfect health, they must take charge of their own lives. I would continue to look after mother financially, on condition that each one of them also contributed to her allowance. After all, there were nine of us, there was no reason why our mother should be dependent on just one. I would sell the Lardy house, as agreed, as I couldn't go on paying all the expenses for them to reduce it to a shambles. I'd give Hakim and Djamila time to find somewhere else to live, but they'd have to move sooner or later. After which I hoped we'd continue to have a proper relationship, the fact of my not being responsible for their board and lodging would not, I hoped, prevent them from having some sense of family solidarity.

They did indeed have a sense of family solidarity. There was a general mobilization against the common enemy: me, of course.

My mother returned from Algeria immediately. She who had decided with me to put the villa up for sale, now declared that there had never been any question of this. Overnight, the house was invaded by the lot of them: brothers and sisters shoulder to shoulder, camping there as if in a state of siege, slamming the door in the face of estate agents, telling them the house didn't belong to me and wasn't for sale. The agencies turned against me and I had to have recourse to legal proceedings to establish the truth.

This situation lasted nearly two years. Two years of

The Veil of Silence

repeated threats, insulting telephone calls, waking Hervé and me up in the middle of the night on our houseboat.

Mohand, as if by chance, decided to return to France, when he'd spent seventeen years in Algiers and had all his professional activities there. Was it the better to direct the operations? To remind me of my 'duties'? What did they all want? For me to continue to house them at my expense? For me to give up Djurdjura, since my sisters were no longer members of the group? For me to continue to hand out money, still more money, as I'd done since the age of twenty – what am I saying – since I was fourteen?

They wanted all that, and much more too. They wanted my ruin, which was not far off, in view of the difficulties which they had created for me. They wanted my professional and emotional downfall. They wanted to get back at me! My sisters were settling their problems of personal jealousy and unsatisfied ambition: if they'd been capable of fully realizing themselves on the professional level, possibly they would have been less vindictive. Some of my brothers reproached me for not paying them to live in idleness any longer, the others for not submitting to their superiority complexes. As for Mohand, he was letting his permanent resentment resurface. Had he not warned me, 'Wherever you are, even in ten years' time or more, I'll find you and kill you . . .'?

My mother was taking it out on me, subconsciously perhaps, for all the sufferings her husband had inflicted on her. And like this husband, who I had substituted in the matter of financial and family responsibilities, she demanded from me – and from me alone – what one has a right to demand from a husband: material security, and even a certain amount of luxury for which she had developed a taste. So she found herself prepared to listen to suggestions from the rest of her children who, knowing she was my weak point, were to set her up against me to the point of no return . . .

The Veil of Silence

One morning, in fact, she appeared suddenly on the towpath where our barge was moored, brandishing her umbrella at me and yelling, 'You want to turn me out, you've kicked your sisters out, all this is the Frenchman's doing, but you'll both pay for it!'

'The Frenchman'! Hervé, who'd done so much for them! My other sisters had henceforth the right to live with anyone they liked, a German or any other foreigner, without the benefit of marriage if need be, but my mother had just reproached with his nationality the only man who had really agreed to help them, claiming that 'all this' (all what?) was his doing!

I tried to calm down this infuriated woman who continued to storm at us from the towpath. I explained that this sacrifice – mine – had lasted long enough, that I had my life to build too.

She stared at me as if I'd just evinced the most outrageous impertinence. My life? Did I even have a life, according to her? She turned on her heels, swearing it would soon go very badly for both of us, we would see what we would see.

Hervé was deathly pale; never could he have thought such an attitude possible. He was ill for several days.

As for me, I didn't know where I was. My mother! The person who was dearest to me in the world, threatening me just as Mohand had done, long ago, in Algiers. I had to try to put things right at all costs, even if I was sure that nothing would ever be the same between us again. I couldn't let her be manipulated in this way by the others. In my innermost heart I was persuaded she did not really love me, although I'd never wanted to admit it . . ., but never that she should begin to hate me, because of them . . .!

I took advantage of Mothers' Day to try to pour oil on troubled waters. I sent her a magnificent multicoloured flower arrangement in a vase with the simple words:

The Veil of Silence

'To my dear Mother.' No doubt she would understand the message.

She understood it in her own way. I proved to her that she still meant much to me, that she could still put pressure on me, triumph cruelly over my weakness where she was concerned . . . The next day I found the vase smashed to smithereens and the flowers trampled on the pavement in front of our old barn, the headquarters of our recording company. Symbolic . . .

This event shattered me. I realized that, throughout my whole life, through all the obligations and acts of generosity I'd imposed on myself, I had merely been looking for a mother's love. Now I had to give up the search: I was an orphan as far as a mother's heart was concerned.

Then, as the saying goes, I cracked up. A euphemism . . . The spring had broken. We were preparing a recording, I could no longer even be bothered with it. I shut myself away in defeatist isolation. I began to lose pounds and pounds in weight, just at the time when I discovered I was pregnant! I tried to take hope again, thanks to this little creature who would console me for my misfortunes, but I was too much in shock, too exhausted, too torn to pieces: I lost my baby.

This miscarriage was the final blow that pushed me over the brink into a deep depression. I had lost everything, whichever way I looked: my mother, my child, my past and my future. So what was the use of struggling to get better?

I struggled nevertheless, subconsciously. At night, I fought against an army of demons in my nightmares. In the morning I prayed to Setsi Fatima to come to my help. I saw little Djura once more, proud, determined, emulating

The Veil of Silence

Kahina the Warrior-Queen. It is said that childhood is the birthplace of the soul: the survival of my willpower sprang from my memories of Ifigha.

Just as when my father had shut me up, for months and months, in Courneuve, I treated myself by reading. Reading has always helped me to understand and accept the dramas of existence. The poems of Nazim Hikmet, a political prisoner, held incommunicado for forty years in Turkey, became my bedside book. I meditated bitterly on his final messages: *'In the twilight of my last morning, I shall see my friends and you, and I shall take under the earth with me nothing but an unfinished song.'*

'My friends and you'? Hervé watched over me tirelessly; all our intimate friends and our musicians surrounded me with a human warmth that would have revived a corpse. They forced me to resume the recording sessions, seated on a stool as I couldn't stand up. Thanks to them, I didn't die and my song did not remain unfinished: my fourth record came out in November 1986.

In a surge of dignity, I called it *'The Challenge'*. An artistic challenge, a human challenge. A challenge to death, and to those who wished me to die. But a smiling challenge, to set against their violence. I was not giving in. I signed: I was continuing on my way.

My family also continued on theirs, and things were far from over. The day the record came out, they returned their own challenge. The headquarters of our company – the old barn which had seen the birth of Djurdjura – was burgled by my brothers, the eldest and the youngest, Mohand and Djamel: in other words, the one who had slashed my face and the one who'd tried his extortion racket on me. A letter from Mohand followed, promising more persecutions.

Numerous objects had been stolen: carpets, screens and other trinkets. But that was not the most serious: administrative documents had been destroyed. Some had

The Veil of Silence

been torn to pieces and scattered on the floor. All our financial records had disappeared, photographs, costumes, press-cuttings, everything had been taken.

We lodged a complaint . . . The police recovered some of the receipts in the basement of the house in Lardy. Nothing else was ever found . . . Brothers, sisters and mother continued to occupy the villa, defying the police and declaring, 'We'll settle this business in our own Algerian fashion.'

I don't think the police could know what that might mean. Neither could Hervé or I have imagined for one minute how far they would go to settle scores.

Despite the more or less explicit threats hanging over us, I had decided not to give in to blackmail any longer. The family coalition had finally opened my eyes. During my whole life, I had been dependent on the affection I felt for my family: their relentless persecution suddenly set me free from this dependency. Now I had to be strong, to build again, create a new family for myself, my future family: Hervé plus a child, should God be willing to grant me another one. I was not actuated by any spirit of revenge. I wanted to forget, and, what is more, to be forgotten.

Only, I was not forgotten: I was surrounded by savages. They prowled around the houseboat to show they were still there, sometimes a brother, sometimes a sister. They would ring up – my mother as well as the others – and threaten, indulge in derisive laughter and hang up abruptly. They waged a veritable war of nerves. I daren't go out any more, I was terrorized.

We had informed the police, but they told us they couldn't do anything as long as there was no real assault. Physical assault. The mental torture to which we were subjected did not fall within the jurisdiction of the security forces.

In an atmosphere like this, my inspiration had a job

to survive. I had composed so many songs denouncing violence, fanaticism, the despotism of men of our lands, with the aim of putting an end to their abominable practices. And there I was, still suffering from these practices, more terribly perhaps than in my adolescence, as if my words, my cries had been of no use to me personally. How could I now offer others hope of possibly reforming these barbaric customs? Where would I find again the constant freshness, the optimism which, despite my critics, used to enliven my poems?

The answer to this question came a few months later when I realized I was once more expecting a baby. It was early in 1987, the finest promise of a 'Happy New Year' . . . I immediately felt myself able to start writing again, to take on shows once more, television programmes, humanitarian causes, the feminist cause. Joy had returned to the house, and too bad about the anonymous phone calls and other warnings!

April 3, for my thirty-eighth birthday, I was showered with gifts and flowers from all my friends who rallied round to express their affection and their loving wishes for the birth of our child, expected in September.

On the afternoon of this party, I learned of the death of my father, from whom I'd parted seventeen years earlier, at the Gare du Nord . . . The fact that he had breathed his last the day before my birthday upset me strangely, and I was sorry I had not seen him again during his lifetime. Something of the tradition remained with me: I would have liked us to meet again before he departed on his final journey, and for us to grant each other mutual forgiveness. That was the correct thing for us to do, and it was good. For, all in all, if my father, by his uncompromising brutality, had ruined my youth, no doubt he too had been unhappy because of me, even if this was the fault of his completely outmoded ideas.

So I was going to have to live without his forgiveness, but I would grant him mine, standing near his mortal remains. However, it was touch and go whether I would be able to see him, even in death . . .

I had been told of his demise by people not related to my family, from whom I also learned that papa had been in hospital in France for some time. My mother, brothers and sisters had been notified of his death, although my father had had virtually no contact with them since his remarriage. But they had decided not to let me know.

When they heard that someone had informed me, they tried to stop me going to the mortuary, backing up their message with the usual threats. However, since they couldn't lay permanent siege to the Medico-Legal Institute, I managed to get in. Hervé stood on guard to make sure none of my family was hanging around. A friend accompanied me, to give me support.

And I saw my father . . . He lay there, behind the glass screen, ashen grey, his features contorted by his final suffering. I said to my friend. 'You see, even now, he frightens me. I'm afraid he'll get up and come and strike me.'

Then I began to weep before this poor man who I could not follow to his last resting place: it was too dangerous for me to go to the funeral. I said, 'Goodbye papa, goodbye papa, goodbye papa,' sixty-two times, once for each year of his life, a doubtless unhappy life for him, to judge by his alcoholic despair and the violence which inhabited him.

But I did not want to think of this misery any more. I granted him my forgiveness, I asked for his in the next world and I repeated, 'May your soul rest in peace, papa' . . .

The Veil of Silence

And I went back to our boat, to the new life I was carrying.

'Djura's expecting a baby!' . . . The news, in the family, must have certainly have had the effect of a bombshell. They would have to have found out sooner or later. I was still performing when four, five then six months pregnant. My condition was obvious, everyone was in the know.

The prospect of the birth of my child most certainly triggered off their final act of insanity: I was escaping from them completely, they could no longer reclaim me, my love would henceforth be bestowed elsewhere.

They continued their acts of intimidation during April and May, by 'phone, in the street, on the towpath. Poisonous snakes. Vipers that I'd nourished in my bosom, that I'd lavished so much love on . . . Conspirators who, although they detested each other, ran each other down, angrily exchanged insults, were able nevertheless to weld the tribe together again as soon as it was a question of defending their heritage, regaining possession of their bread-winner: me.

In this monstrous vendetta, Hervé served as scapegoat. According to them, he was the one who had led me astray, who had influenced me in my decision to give up supporting them, which was absolutely false. 'He was the one who owned the goodwill of the company,' they were to state later, at the trial.

Be that as it may, once my companion and I had refused to ruin ourselves any more for them, and had dared to reserve our largesse for a yet unborn child, we were going to 'pay for it' as my mother had said. We remained on the alert, expecting more burglaries, more attempts at extortion, some ransacking of our company office or our home, but certainly not what was to occur on 29 June.

The Veil of Silence

An abomination. A punitive expedition decided on by the clan, their envoys being my brother Djamel and my niece Sabine.

I had not seen Sabine, Mohand's daughter, again since he had brought her for me to mind in my bedsit-prison in Hussen Dey. It was when Djamel, armed with his revolver, had called to her from the stairway of the houseboat, that I realized who she was. Sabine! One more infant whose nappies I'd changed, like Djamel who had just dragged her into this retaliatory operation.

I discovered later that these two saw a great deal of each other, as Sabine had been living in Paris for some time already. They hung out with the same devil-may-care bunch of cronies, smoking pot, pulling off fairly risky jobs.

And now, here I was, lying in a hospital bed, reliving the horror of their latest outrage. However much I tried to drive this terrible memory out of my mind, I could still see Djamel bursting into our little home, pointing his revolver at my stomach, then beating Hervé up. I could still hear the sound of the shot up on deck, and I was haunted by the sight of my bleeding, wounded companion. I could still feel the kicks that my niece aimed at my unborn baby as well as at me.

Immediately I thought of this little creature who they had not succeeded in destroying, but who was still in danger. Then I breathed deeply, I calmed down, I gathered my courage together . . . I looked at Hervé, leaning over me, frighteningly pale, with a wound in his skull, with stitches in his forehead and nose, obliged to wear a neck-brace . . .

And I could not understand the leniency that had allowed the two assailants to go free! For they had been caught in the act – by an extraordinary chance.

On that scorching June afternoon, the surroundings of

The Veil of Silence

the houseboat were deserted. Well, nearly . . . In fact, after Djamel had shot at Hervé, a witness had seen him running away, followed by my niece. And what a witness! A police inspector in plain clothes, out for a walk alone along the towpath.

Heaven-sent, when you come to think about it. For it is true I had myself phoned Police-Emergencies, but by the time they arrived the two culprits would have been far away and I would never have been able to prove that they were the attackers. The inspector who was taking his stroll, seeing these two fugitives covered with blood, had chased after them. He hadn't managed to catch Djamel; my brother had slipped through his fingers by threatening him with his weapon, but he had been seen. The inspector had however been able to arrest Sabine and put the handcuffs on her.

Djamel, guessing that sooner or later Sabine would denounce him, and also – I suppose – on the advice of the rest of the family, gave himself up at the police station, certain that this 'show of remorse' would act in his favour. Result: after a night's interrogation, both accomplices were released on bail, while awaiting trial.

They telephoned us without delay, 'We're out! Justice is on our side: you'll be seeing us soon!'

Were they going to be able to lay down the law with impunity *ad vitam*? No-one had been killed, true enough, but Hervé had been violently struck on the head, he had been seriously wounded, I had been beaten black and blue and maybe my child would not survive this destructive fury. Would the court consider this 'incident' as simply a 'family affair'? Moreover, justice functions in slow gear, especially in summer; would these maniacs leave me in peace, while waiting for the verdict?

Hervé begged me not to lose myself in these conjectures; to think of our child. But I remained a long time in shock.

The Veil of Silence

The slightest sound – of a car, of a motor-bike back-firing, a rumble of thunder – made me jump . . .

As soon as it was possible, Hervé took me far away from Paris to a place kept secret from everybody, and watched over me until our baby was born. But in the meantime he insisted we get married. Up till now, we both used to say with a laugh, 'We are each other's prisoners "on parole".' But times had changed.

'Just imagine,' he said, 'if Djamel had killed me. Our child would have been born of an unknown father and your family would have managed somehow to lay hands on him. We can't run that risk any more.'

And so, one fine morning, we made our way to the Mayor's parlour, and then returned discreetly to our secret hiding-place. Hervé never left my side. He tried to soothe me, always with a smile on his lips, picking up his guitar and singing Brassens's songs to me: *'Draw the curtain, sweetheart, shut out the heartbreak and the pain. Draw the curtain on the stormy weather, ignore the wind and the rain.'*

4 September 1987, there were no storms; it was a lovely day: my son had just been born. For several months I remained entranced, like mothers the world over, with his exceptional beauty and the remarkable intelligence he already displayed in his cradle!

Then we really had to resurface. We couldn't remain buried like that forever, anonymous and unoccupied, in adoration of our latest creation. We had to make new programmes for concerts, resume a 'normal' life, if you can use that adjective when you feel constantly in danger.

So we went back to the boat, well aware that 'the others' still existed . . . However, for my husband as for me, terror

The Veil of Silence

had given way to the instinct for self-defence. The police had told us, 'We are wholeheartedly on your side, but we can't protect you twenty-four hours a day.' Be that as it may, there had to be other ways of protecting ourselves. We were advised to employ bodyguards, to ask permission to carry a weapon, to . . . Hervé opted, in my opinion, for a combination of the most appropriate precautions, which I shall not divulge for obvious reasons, not wishing to reveal our trump cards to our crazy enemies.

Meanwhile, Djamel had been sentenced to eighteen months imprisonment and Sabine to six. They appealed and my brother's sentence was reduced to ten months without remission and two years on probation, plus a fine of a hundred thousand francs, payable at the rate of . . . five hundred francs a month. Sabine, for her part, didn't go to prison; she put on so good a show, acting the sentimental drama of the little girl led astray in spite of herself, that she got off with a fine of ten thousand francs, and six months suspended sentence.

It was not a lot for so much violence, but the trial had a certain advantage all the same: in view of the publicity given to the clan's objectives, the law would henceforth have its eye on my family, and in case of any backsliding, they wouldn't be dealt with so leniently. My persecutors understood: there were no more attacks.

But that did not prevent them getting at me in another way, that is, by suing us on the most far-fetched grounds! I, who had never set foot in a court of law before the 'affair' with Djamel and Sabine, I was now in it up to my neck! Writs flew every which way. My mother, my

The Veil of Silence

brothers, my sisters claimed money, allowances, additional fees. Furthermore, they tried to get an injunction prohibiting me from singing, while demanding royalties on my music and words, which they claimed they had written. They had all become author-composers! Even Djamel, who alleged he had written my songs since the beginning of Djurdjura, when he was only thirteen at the time!

My sisters brought proceedings against me in the Industrial Conciliation Court, still obsessed with the idea that I was their employer. My mother, caught up in her contradictory grievances, also swore she had composed my poems. Then she brought a charge against me for 'forging signatures' on the grounds that I had signed documents in her name. Obviously, I had signed documents in her name! Ever since I was twelve, with Social Security, for Family Allowances, in all dealings with administration, since she couldn't do this herself, being totally unable to read or write.

Some of these lawsuits are not yet finished. I have won all the ones that are over, and what is more I obtained the possibility of regaining possession of the house in Lardy.

Only, what a waste of so much time and energy! So much suffering stirred up at each confrontation! I wanted all that to end. I refused to let the complications of my past totally dominate the present, now that a little boy at my side smiled towards the future. But by what means could I wipe out all my suffering?

Since I could not go to Ifigha to recharge my batteries, as I was prohibited from entering Algeria, I went to the

The Veil of Silence

Château de Calan in Brittany to meditate. In this oriental edifice, re-named Keer Moor – 'The House by the Sea' – I turned my thoughts once more to Setsi Fatima who used to call me her 'bright shining rose' or 'plaything of love'. Was I going to let myself be overwhelmed by the dark shadows of my tragic memories and lose my ability to love?

I also thought of Tahar again, the marabout my grandmother and I had gone to consult, and who had given me a sprig of mint, saying 'You will be luminous Djura!'

I begged both of them to restore the light to me, to bring about the miracle which would eradicate from my heart the evil which was eroding it.

For it was indeed a question . . . of evil: the pain inside me was like a poison. I did not want it to be transformed into bitterness, into a wish to avenge myself on those who had persecuted me so fiercely. I wanted this pain within me to pour out, for me to express it once and for all and be rid of it.

Setsi Fatima and the old sage decided no doubt to inspire me with the solution which would set me free: to entrust to my pen my emotions, tears, struggles, but also the fantastic world of legends and history from which I come.

I was by no means out to settle scores with my family in my turn. So I have written my life-story as simply as possible, without any vindictive diatribes, demystifying page by page those who were my masters, my persecutors, my ogres, but who I refused to let become ghosts to haunt me. I swept away rancour and sorrow, without any wish to dwell on the well-nigh criminal ingratitude of which I had been the victim. 'Do good and then forget it,' says the Arabic proverb. I have forgotten while writing.

The Veil of Silence

I still love my mother, even if she will never reciprocate this love. And if someone reads these pages to her, I want her to know that it is also for her, among others, that I have bared this tearful soul.

For you, mother, and for all those women like you who were forced into marriage, obliged to submit to the brutal rages of their spouses, hardened to ancestral violence, but who nevertheless imposed on them their 'natural' desires. For all the Norahs, Zohras, Fatimas, who were disowned or killed if they fled. For all the girls brought up in France but who, once they reached marriageable age, were sent back home, ostensibly for a holiday, when in fact the family simply wanted to marry them off to a man of their choice, and who couldn't leave again because their papers had been confiscated.

For the immigrant women who come at the end of my performances to confide in me their misfortunes or their tragedies. These often suffer a double scourge. On the one hand they face the horrors of racism all around them, which is part xenophobia and part fear of delinquency, whereas delinquents are not always aliens – far from it! On the other hand, more often than you think, they are confronted with the demands of an obtuse tradition, over which even Arab poets are divided. The one says, 'Remove your veil, rend it and bury it in the grave.' The other exclaims, 'I challenge in God's name that idea of progress which wishes to remove the veil from the chaste faces of our women,' as if chastity relied on a piece of cloth. Chastity, loyalty too, obey much more exacting masters: they depend on ethics and love. Do our male friends realize this?

I nurse the very foolhardy hope, in fact, that some men

The Veil of Silence

of my race, of my religion and of my country will read these lines without complaining of women's subversion, licentiousness, hostility. We do not hate them, we do not want to betray them. But they should know that, if they hope to be cherished and made much of as they would wish, they should first leave us free to decide on our social, professional and sentimental lives.

I also express the wish that my native Algeria, after having fought for independence, should make progress towards democracy. Then I shall have the joy of returning there to sing of my primary concern: *Tilleli*, this word which re-echoes in my heart like the flight of a bird, *tilleli*, freedom! The freedom to express and confront one's opinions, the freedom to unite in friendship or love with the one they call a foreigner. Foreigner by civil status, not to mention by religion: let them all be free to practise the religion of their choice, or not as the case may be, without banishing from their world those who do not share their imperfect certainties.

I shall continue to sing of this foolish hope of harmony for my son's generation. It is true, this book is but a minute brick in a most fragile edifice, but I hope that the testimony which it brings – among others – will help the children of the same age as my little boy, children born in France or elsewhere, in a single culture or a multicultural society, not to propagate the dangerous fear of The Other. For it is that fear which is at the root of hatred: fear of what is different, that difference which is a source of enrichment but which still so terrifies human beings that it prevents them from trying to understand, and thus to love, or at the least to live without conflict.

The Veil of Silence

My son's name is Riwan. In the Berber language that means 'Child of Music'. In the Brittany of King Arthur and the Round Table, it means 'The King Who Advances'.

Riwan is a Berber-Breton.